WITHDRAWN W9-ADC-169

Street
Baldwinsville, NY 13027-2575

JUN 1 7 2020

Baldwinsville Public Library
33 East Genesee Street
WITHDRAWN 575

DAVID LAZAR

A NOVEL

BY ROBERT KALICH

BUNIM & BANNIGAN PUBLISHERS
MONTREAL, CANADA

JUN 1 7 2020

Copyright © Robert Alan Kalich, 2019

All rights reserved. No part of this book may be reproduced or transmitted in any form or by any means, electronic or mechanical, including photographing, recording, or by any information storage and retrieval system, without permission in writing from the publisher.

Published in North America in 2019 by

Bunim & Bannigan Ltd.
P.O. Box 72131 BP Atwater
Montreal, QC
H3J2Z6
Canada

www.bunimandbannigan.com

Library and Archives Canada Cataloguing in Publication

Title: David Lazar : A Novel / Robert Kalich.
Names: Kalich, Robert Allen, 1937– author.
Identifiers: Canadiana 20190143606 | ISBN 9781933480497 (hardcover)
Classification: LCC PS3561.A425 D38 2019 | DDC 813/.54—dc23

Design by Rita Lascaro

Printed in Canada

For my wife Brunde and Knute, my son.

With appreciation to those who assisted, motivated, and helped: people like Merle Drown, my Maxwell Perkins; Angelo Pastoramerlo, my left arm; Meryl Zegarek, my confidant; and to my twin brother Richard Barry Kalich, who is everything.

A true story with blurred lines between fiction and memoir to protect the confidentiality of each person fleshed out and characterized . . .

In the real world, motives are mixed. People are unreliable. There are contradictions. People forget. There are omissions. You certainly don't know everything. There aren't good people and bad people. There are shades of this and that.
　　　　—William H. Gass

Life can only be understood backwards; but it must be lived forwards.
　　　　—Søren Kierkegaard

Try not to become a man of success, but rather try to become a man of value.
　　　　—Albert Einstein

We're all mixed bags.
　　　　—Gordon Gekko

AN OMEN FROM THE AUTHOR

The protagonist is not likeable. He is unlikeable. He has inimical traits stretching the worldly gamut from Here to There. Those traits take center stage when he whines and feels sorry for himself rather than man up and offer remorse to those individuals he manipulated, maimed, and destroyed. To add pepper to his cruelties, David Lazar's lifestyle should be labeled obscene, an eighty-year stench. Let's face it, David Lazar is not to be envied. He's as universally flawed as most of us. Read on; decide for yourself if I am mistaken.

PROLOGUE

On two of the high walls of my wood-paneled study are giant collages with extremely small photographs of faces pasted onto cardboards. When I look at this collage of people, I see my own life in front of me as if it were beginning and ending, living with deep gulps of nostalgia, heartache, and self-condemnation in between. Think of it as taking a swim in dangerous currents, going under, coming back to the surface to gasp one more time. It all began so long ago.

But this is not a story going from point to point; instead, it's a shuffling of my entire existence, like a deck of cards. So, if I confuse you, it just happens to be the way I see my life, not as anything coherent or straightforward but as cards being manipulated by a dealer's deft hands, falling into place as if they were casino chips and when stacked—Bingo! You have an octogenarian who's still surviving, some would say, on God's inexplicable blessed air.

The question now is, can you place these cards of my life where they belong?

CHAPTER 1

It's a glorious day. From the bedroom window, I can see leaves falling to the ground. Scattering, predictably gathering in bunches, as children do in a school playground. I head for the breakfast nook I am so fond of. Scoop the *New York Times* off the kitchen table and take stock of the kitchen. After all these Westchester County years, I still can't believe its size. Amazingly, such considerations as comfort, coziness, convenience, accoutrements—I've evolved into a serious collector of first editions and outsider art—have become more than mere indulgences. The imported marble kitchen tabletops, the gleaming white-tiled walls, the magnificent antiques, the furniture and furnishings, the George P.A. Healy 1869 painting of Lincoln, the verdant views . . . these trappings force me to think of antithetical Harlem, its penniless unending powerlessness. Never did I find a breath of fresh air in the Apollo Theatre, Rucker Park, the reconditioned brownstones, cleaner streets, more attractive storefronts. Still in my head are welfare clients that I served there, nearly sixty years ago. The Rivera family, Mike Tafuri, Mr. and Mrs. Hodapp. Eloise Goyens. Fourteen-year-old Gabriella Blanco. Fifty-two East 118th Street. Swaying not-so-young women play-acting whores: "Hey mister! Want a blow job? $3!"

And there, but for the grace of my skin color and the serendipity of birth, go I.

Color and situation still matter in this absurd world of ours. Money, even more. I made dollars because of my good fortune or luck or aberrational skills or whatever you want to label it. I did make money. I did Make It.

I start the day by brewing myself a fresh pot of coffee, adding cream, drinking fresh orange juice, scrambling a few eggs, going through the *Times Book Review* section. I'm ready for the "I love you" between Elizabeth and I, which, still, after two decades of marriage, doesn't feel obligatory. I assumed we would speak about what to tell our son Liam, if anything, about things that I had never mentioned.

Without any prompting from Elizabeth, I have dwelled for months on how much to tell my son. For sure, we'll also speak about his robotics projects and about some of the colleges that he is applying to. Liam is partial to Stanford in the West, Princeton in the East. And I wouldn't forget to mention to Elizabeth that Liam had texted me searching for his sandals.

Elizabeth enters the kitchen holding a porcelain cup of steaming black coffee. Her hands are shaking. The cup is rattling on the saucer. Liz is wearing my navy blue, cashmere bathrobe and my son's sandals. Before I can utter a word, she is sobbing. Slowly at first. Then faster.

"I was up most of the night," she says. "I read your memoir, from cover to cover." She stops and wipes a tear from her cheek. "Before you say a word, I realize what you sacrificed for me during these last twenty years. How difficult it was for you to become domesticated." She stops again. "We must talk, David."

I see the same sorrowful eyes that had gazed at me when I brought her home after our first date, and she said, "I've never been happy a single day in my entire life."

At that moment, something inside me opened. I wanted to convert Elizabeth's pain into something joyous. I wanted her to experience delight, fun, as I had growing up, my PM Two baseball glove, kosher food, books.

"Maybe it's me." Elizabeth sobs. "I think I have always denied who you really are. I psyched myself into believing that you were someone I had always wanted you to be. A magical elixir or healer, and so delicious that one's always craving for more. You're exciting. You're smart. You're different. You're like that pitcher, Bob Gibson, who couldn't throw a straight pitch. You're always throwing a pitch that's darting around and diving. You must have struck me out every day for all these years."

Elizabeth bites her lip, stammers, "Evan Strome!"

"That's one of the things in the manuscript that isn't true. One day Evan just disappeared. I didn't threaten him or give him any ultimatums. I certainly didn't place a contract out on him."

"And you didn't hunt him down?"

"I have no hard feelings for Evan Strome. He was a hell of a lot like me."

What amazes me is how I have learned to lie so adroitly to Elizabeth. So, when she asked questions, I circumvented truthful answers and found it very easy to tell her bold-faced lies and play the role of the thunder headed Dad.

I remain mute while I try to figure out what I can say to salvage my marriage. Keep my son.

"You're right, Elizabeth!" I said. "I just didn't want to help Evan Strome. Something inside of me stopped me." I begin to throw out hollow justifications for my actions. "You know how I am, Elizabeth, when I think I'm right, I just don't change my mind. With Evan Strome, I simply didn't want to help him. He—"

I stop. I can see that Elizabeth isn't buying any of this. Then I make a terrible mistake. Rather than tell the truth or explain the deep sorrow I feel, I begin to articulate the reasons I thought Evan Strome was rotten. I don't include myself in this judgment. It's only Strome I condemn.

"David, I think you're very sick," Elizabeth says in an almost pitying voice.

I don't utter a sound.

"You're sick, David."

"You're right," I mutter.

I gaze at Elizabeth's well-meaning face. Her furrowed brow. She's chewing on the lapel of my bathrobe.

"I don't know what I'm going to do," she says.

I make every effort to remember that Liz is my wife! My companion! My best friend! The woman I love! I try extra hard to think of Liam.

Elizabeth starts to chastise me again, and the more she does, the more I keep insisting that I would do it all over again. The same way.

CHAPTER 2

I'm looking at my collages. On one board are people alive with memories of yesterday; on the other wall are hindsights—let's call them bottom-line realities—of what went right or wrong or maybe nowhere in particular. Each day, the collages are colliding. After Elizabeth's question about Evan Strome, the dynamics are changing. Each day I think about what, if anything, to tell her, to tell Liam.

The arrangement of the collages should reveal beginnings, endings. Vague memories. Obscene realities. Flashes of what is or was or still can be. A black comedy of regurgitations on yesterday's experiences, today's brief tweets. Will I learn enough to decide what to reveal, what to hide?

The only thing I'm sure of is that when I look at this collage of people, I see my own life in front of me, beginning to end. My grandfather pushing my baby carriage on Eastern Parkway. Being four years old and riding in my dad's Dodge into congested Manhattan, where we took up residence on 106th Street and West End Avenue. We lived in one of those winding three-bedroom apartments with a massive foyer and huge bay windows overlooking Riverside Drive, the Hudson River. My loving parents would say, "There's the *Queen Mary*...That's the *Queen Elizabeth*...Here comes the triple-stacked *SS Normandie*. It was built in Saint-Nazaire, France, David. Its length is 1,029 feet. It was launched October 29, 1932." These giant-sized ocean liners passed by our dining room and living room windows before moving south toward the larger sea. After a while, I identified these ships by their smokestacks and by my parents' unbridled excitement as they repeated their historical biographies. The *Normandie* caught fire and capsized in 1942. I was five years old and wept for two whole days.

I could even see Palisades Amusement Park from our windows. We were on the top floor on a quiet block far from the "toughie" side of our neighborhood, which was only blocks east of where the growing Hispanic population was quickly becoming part of the melting pot.

One week after we moved to the Upper West Side, my mother took me to Radio City Music Hall to see the Disney film *Bambi*, and I was crying, giggling, and glowing.

I delve into my life with a rusty nail. I have flashes of working for the Department of Welfare as a caseworker. We were called Social Investigators back in September of 1958 when I started to work in a white-bricked building on 131st Street and Park Avenue. I had no idea what I was going to do with my life. I had turned down my father's offer.

"David—I have an opportunity to buy into a very successful catering business. You'll have something solid!"

"Are you crazy, Dad? The last thing I want to do is be a businessman."

We went to housing projects like 350 East 124th Street whose residents needed more than we could ever provide. I was pure of heart, a well-intentioned boy with an honorable dad and a mother even more decent than my father the cantor.

At twenty-one, I walked to the front of the building, stepped over a strung-out woman, and entered the lobby. Two drug guys were dealing. They reached for weapons. I flashed them my black field book and hoped that they would know I was working for Welfare. (A co-worker, Norma Meyers, had advised me to do that.) They returned to selling drugs, and I kept moving. I knocked on a door to visit the first client of a thousand I would see over the next three years.

Here in my office, I begin to cry.

Not over a photograph on a wall. Not part of my two collages. Flashes of people that I had helped in 1958. Why them and not the extraordinary people, good friends or close relatives or the many I bounced with or had intimate relationships with or the many I bumped into on an almost daily basis, like, say, Albert Rolon, a handyman in my building, or Tim Brown, the silver-haired maître de at Porterhouse? People I can fill a book with? People I will fill a book with?

Because these people from 1958 make me feel good about myself.

The Welfare Department assigned me about ninety cases. That winter I had clients at the Wagner Projects and all over East Harlem. I met people. Henry and Edith Hodapp. Edith was born in 1888; Henry in 1877.

Those birth dates seemed ancient to me in 1958. Now I'm Henry's age. The Hodapps were humble, polite, gentle people. A lifetime couple without children. They resided at 2405 2nd Avenue. (I'm still good with numbers. Helped me with handicapping. Not sure it will do me any good handicapping what to tell Elizabeth.) I visited the Hodapps regularly that winter and usually stayed a long while. It was always just the two of them, inseparable in that way people connected with each other in those days were. Neither one ever complained about their circumstances. They didn't have a TV though their Emerson radio was always playing. They never mentioned the old country or anyone from their past. Henry was bald and toothless with a craggy face. I never saw him smile. I neglected to ask him what he did in his prime. I imagine it had been something physical like carpentry or plowing furrows in arid land. Maybe he had driven a horse and wagon. Edith was tiny, snow-haired, and quiet. She looked like a winter sparrow all balled up and ready to perish, but Edith didn't perish that winter. She was feisty and in charge of her husband's welfare. She even questioned me about my future.

"Mrs. Hodapp, I had a long talk with my mother. She feels that I should continue for a master's in journalism at Columbia. I'm not sure I can do that and still hold this job here."

"You should try to do both, Mr. Lazar. You know how it is. Where there's a will, there's a way."

I liked Edith Hodapp a lot.

Winter came in June as Edith quickly and quietly passed away. I visited Henry Hodapp on late afternoons, mostly on Fridays after I had finished with my other clients. His face held even deeper crevices, more wrinkles. His azure blue eyes were always watery, sometimes streaming. Without his wife, he ate oatmeal, string beans, a slice of Velveeta; his dinners simply warmed white bread covered with mayonnaise. The last time I visited Mr. Hodapp, he said, "I've accepted that Edith's gone. I'm ready to join her."

Mike Tafuri was one of my all-time favorite people during my Welfare years. I'd make a special effort to end my day by checking in on him. I'd stay with him an extra half hour or so, which was a big deal as most of the Social Investigators left the field as early as they could.

Mike was born in 1869. He lived at the Gaylord White Houses at 2029 2nd Avenue. A tough little guy with a history. He'd worked for the mob when he was younger.

"Mr. Lazar, I remember things." And then he would tell me stories, squinting out each word from his grey-blue eyes. "Mr. Lazar," he'd say, "Don't ever end up like me."

Some of those people looked after me as much as I looked after them.

Some of my clients had tragic lives. Eloise Goyens, a twenty-two-year-old woman from Tampa, relocated with her twin daughters to 112th Street and Park Avenue in East Harlem. A comely woman, she amazed me by how forthcoming she was in telling me her horrific story.

"I left Tampa, Mr. Lazar, because the man I was living with was always shootin' up and in bad temper. More than that, Mr. Lazar, he was always puttin' his hands on my girls."

The last day I saw her, I felt I had helped her move to a hopeful and better life.

"Mr. Lazar," she said, "I went to church last Sunday and let me tell you, I prayed real hard. Now I'm ready to sign up for that program we discussed. Mr. Lazar, I want to do right for people like me. I want to be a childcare worker."

Eloise Goyens could have been the daughter my mother had always prayed for. She could have been family. Then one morning just before Christmas, I was riding the subway uptown to the Welfare office and reading *The Herald Tribune* and I saw, "Woman and six-year-old twin daughters found dead."

The man from Tampa had hunted Eloise down and cut her throat and the throats of her two girls.

A year later I was still working for the Welfare Department. I had interviewed for positions with *The New York Times*, *The New Yorker* magazine, even with the Yankees and the Knickerbockers. I failed each time. So, to make ends meet, I kept my job with Welfare. When I was growing up, I was unaware that there was such a thing as the civil service. My mom's friends all had degrees, some doctorates. My father's colleagues were either opera superstars like Jan Pearce and Richard Tucker or religious cantors the likes of Louis Waldman, Arnold Diamond, Moshe Koussevitzky or saturnine businessmen, members of his congregation who only took seriously their balance sheets and their God. For my bar mitzvah, Richard Tucker gave me a PM Two baseball glove, the greatest present in the world I thought at the time. One young man in my father's congregation wrote comedy scripts for Fred Allen, my mother told me. Years later I learned it was Herman Wouk, the novelist.

Such a different world from that of my Welfare clients. Most of my caseload were Aid to Dependent Children families. Some were disabled individuals. Some the elderly, classified as "O.A.A."—Old Age Assistance. A few were Home Reliefs. Two or three were felony addicts from Rikers Island jail. Drugs, violent sex abusers, and limb amputations were abundant. With Social Investigators, what you saw was what there was in New York at midday. Very few cared . . .

I did what I could. I was no hero. I too dreamed of a better life. Each week two or three pendings (new cases) crossed my desk. Most of the workers bitched at the extra work. No one in civil service was entrepreneurial. The social investigator caseworker had to read policy and familiarize himself with stuff that took a miniscule amount of intellect. Policy, familiarity, and execution. And at times, a supervisor or a case supervisor had to intervene. For me, it was as easy as taking an exam that required me to name the starting center for the championship 1959 Boston Celtics (Bill Russell).

One day my Viennese supervisor, Hans Neurath, assigned me a pending. "David, it would be a kindness if you visited this case immediately. The family is in trouble: three children, two boys, a little girl, ages from two to eleven. No man in the house. A woman both physically hurt and mentally abused."

What did I know? I was a Jewish kid from a middle-class home. My parents never prepared me for this reality. There I was, hardly shaving more than twice a week, going into the field to visit four broken people. I was thinking on the way home I'd stop at Mr. Pollock's candy store for a chocolate milkshake with pretzels. I was also thinking of my mother's home cooking, Friday night's rib steak with so much else loaded on the dining room table. That's what I was thinking as I headed over to the Wagner Projects in East Harlem to visit Latoya Earl and her children.

I knocked on the door, and an emaciated boy opened it. I entered the project apartment and looked around. One look. Two. I quickly moved from room to room. In the bedroom there was nothing but two filthy mattresses oozing stuffing. In the kitchen I opened the fridge. Nothing there but ice. Inside a closet I found one pair of jeans hanging on a hook. I returned to the bedroom. Looked under the mattresses. Three pairs of shoes. Cardboard for soles.

Tommy, the emaciated eleven-year-old said, "Mister, the reason our shoes are under the mattresses is that it keeps them warm. We haven't had any heat in three weeks."

When I checked out a second closet, a rat the size of my foot ran out. Inside the closet were rat droppings and a Rangers sweatshirt with a large hole in it hanging on a hook. I moved to the bathroom. The toilet was stuffed.

I raced out of Mrs. Earl's apartment into a creaking elevator. Rushed out onto the icy street where the wind chill was below zero. I found a working payphone on 123rd Street and Paladino Avenue and called my supervisor.

"David, do what you can. You know city policy. No emergency grants can be given without writing up the case, and we must submit it and get approval from a case supervisor for what you are requesting. Just write it up when you come in Monday morning, and we'll discuss it Tuesday afternoon."

"Screw this!" I mumbled under my breath. (I would say that to myself countless times in the nightmare Welfare years in my future.) On that day, I telephoned my mom.

"Mom, do you have any cash in the house? I need to buy some winter coats, shoes and warm socks, blankets, food for a family of four." That's how my two-year casework/friendship with Latoya Earl and her three children started.

CHAPTER 3

I met Solomon Lepidus in 1961 when I was twenty-four, and it changed my life. From the day I met him until the day he died, Thanksgiving Day, 1989, for all those twenty-eight years, I was captivated and seduced by him. Solomon Lepidus was not only the action hero my father wasn't but he led an army of employees, some of them just out of prison. He took men out of some dark and unforgiving somewhere and saved their lives or gave them back their lives or protected them from losing their lives. He was also a retrograde gambler and a whole lot of other not so law-abiding things.

On my collage I see him, a picture of a mob-connected, street smart, sociopathic New Yorker in the 1960s. One who grew up on the violent streets of the Bronx with gangsters like Frank Costello. "Davey boy," Solomon would say to me, "the kids in my neighborhood didn't know they were poor. We played baseball with sticks. Didn't have money for Spaldings. We were all in the same boat back then. After high school, the smartest kids on the block took the post office test. The dumb ones, like me, we went to work for $6 a week. That's how come I started working on a jewelry bench."

Solomon Lepidus wore thick glasses, was stocky, and extra wide. He might have been mistaken for Ernest Borgnine playing "Marty," until he opened his mouth. His voice was raspy, deep down in his throat, his vocabulary was colorful, his inflection New Yorkese, and he always had an opinion. I met Solomon Lepidus through Hana Aroni, his mistress. At the time, I thought that Israeli woman was the most beautiful woman I had ever seen. Still do. I met Hana at The Toast, a singles bar on the Upper Eastside of Manhattan. Within a week, she introduced me to Solomon. She and I had an affair, but Hana was only interested in Solomon.

Hana worked as a nurse's aide until Solomon Lepidus extricated her from bacteria and dung. As humble as Hana's beginnings were, beauty like hers has its own vertical voyage. Once Hana was exposed to

Solomon's wise guy and CEO crowd, guys became unhinged over her. Every man's doors were wide open to her. But it was Solomon Lepidus who had nailed Hana Aroni to his green-dollar-cross and who told most of the men who were interested, "Stay off the grass."

I liked Hana Aroni as a person, but I was never smitten with her. Solomon Lepidus was. He never stopped pumping me for my thoughts on his concubine. "Do you think Hana really loves me?" or "Where does she get the strength. I just spent two hours with her and believe me, Davey boy, I did my job, and now she's going out with you tonight."

There wasn't a day that went by that I wasn't aware that Solomon Lepidus was a walking contradiction: from making millions to giving away millions to being friends with the gangster Frank Costello. One night at his steakhouse, when I criticized "the prime minister," Solomon stood up at his table and in front of an overflow crowd roared at me, "Frank Costello is a great American. He's saved thousands of lives."

Solomon couldn't see that he was a walking contradiction. Of course, so was I and, more often than not, I couldn't see it either. Nor had Elizabeth, until recently, though she recognized it in Solomon even though he was dead before she and I met.

Solomon Lepidus was always in bad faith. He was the most spiritually diminished man I knew. Not a word he said could you hold onto. Not a thought that didn't have two meanings. Solomon helped everyone. He took advantage of everyone. He was the kind of instrumentalized soul that can only be quantified. If you looked deeper into his agenda, you would find nothing but springs, wires and, ultimately, atrocities. He lived in two worlds: to those he protected, he was a champion amongst men; to those he wasted, he was the devil.

He was my best friend. My partner. Handicapping college basketball games was an art form as well as a profession to me. To him, gambling was a luxury he could afford to get high on. If I made Solomon Lepidus a hundred thousand, or even more, what did it matter? He'd only find a way to piss it away. It wasn't the money that he lost gambling that angered me. It was his total disregard for the work I put in to make him that money. Solomon Lepidus was Martin Buber's I-It. I wanted I-Thou. When I worked in welfare, I was I-Thou, but when I turned to handicapping, I, too, became I-It. I lived as corrupt a life as Solomon. More so! Because I knew every minute what it was I was defiling. Solomon didn't. He was libidinal, instinctive, Eros incarnate. I was cerebral. I didn't numb my brain, only my soul.

In 1961 I also hung out with the promoter, Stickers. He got his sobriquet when he was sixteen and promoting his first dance. He had cut up paper and stuck "Stickers Presents" on every car windshield from 161st Street and River Avenue to 96th Street and Park. The dance was a huge success, and for the next three score and eleven years, Stickers promoted and presented just about everyone in the music business.

Stickers was 355 pounds of lard, and during the hot New York summer he would drag me down to the iconic music club The Bitter End on Wednesday nights so he could scout talent. He was always searching for artists to manage or promote, make a score with. He found more than his share, yet it didn't work out most of the time. We would start our evenings off at Serendipity III on 60th Street between 2nd and 3rd Avenues. Stickers would begin with the house favorite, a frozen hot chocolate, then an ice cream sundae, then a thick vanilla malted, then a large bowl of strawberry and vanilla or coffee ice cream with three cherries on top and one kind or another of a chocolate chip cookie. If it weren't the chocolate chip, it would be cheesecake or layer cake, and Stickers, being a conscientious friend, would always request, "Two long, skinny spoons, please. One for my friend and one for me." I hardly ever joined in.

1961 was the year Mickey Mantle and Roger Maris chased Babe Ruth's home-run record. I see the headline when Maris beat it with "61" on my collage. 1961 was a sea change for me. I hit a home run when I left Welfare for a job on the *New York Daily Mirror*. It was the year that I lived at 356 West 56th Street, in Manhattan. The six-story building had white bricks, a wobbly elevator, and several fire escapes out front facing the Parc Vendome.

The one-bedroom apartment was $156 a month, a whole lot more than I could afford on my $48 a week salary. Though the *Mirror* was a crummy tabloid, to me it was a great newspaper. I worked with hard-boiled, black-coffee-newspaper guys. Aileen Mehle, aka "Suzy," gossip's grande dame, Selig Adler, Dan Parker, Lee Mortimer, Walter Winchell—that's correct, Winchell. I mainly worked for Wicked Walter's formidable girl Friday, Rose Bigman, and sometimes, because of good fortune, I was allowed to cover celebrity parties. A Page Six type of fantasy job it was. Anyway, I was sitting next to the stout William Randolph Hearst Jr., and near the glamorous Suzy, and dating the captivating Leslie Kore.

As I told Elizabeth, the only thing I'd change about my life is that I'd never have anything to do with Leslie Kore. Such an idea didn't occur to me in 1961 when I was sleeping with her.

On Sundays, Max Asnas' Stage Deli would serve a thick giblet soup for one dollar. All of my gang counted the days til Sunday when we could slurp that giblet soup at the Stage. You could meet comics there like Dick Shawn and Morty Gunty and Jackie Mason and Henny "Take My Wife . . . Please!" Youngman; crooners like Steve Lawrence and Bobby Darin and Tony Bennett; actors like Jason Robards and Jerry Orbach. I loved those days. I was broke, and I was meeting all kinds of celebrities and sleeping with Leslie Kore. Leslie had already modeled in front of a white Cadillac in a national magazine ad, showed off her shoulder length chestnut hair in TV commercials, and been plastered on billboards all over the East Coast for a cigarette commercial. She'd been married at least twice, and things were hedonistic and wild and . . . Yes! Although it was shallow of me, I loved seeing all those grizzled old-school *New York Daily Mirror* newspapermen getting aroused every time Leslie Kore made one of her spectacular appearances in the editorial offices to pick me up for lunch.

But I couldn't afford the $156 rent. That's where it paid to have a best friend as generous as Santa. Ron Nevins was my closest friend, the one who had anointed me Broadway Dave because of all the fabulous women I had been meeting and dating. A Dartmouth grad, Ron Nevins lived with his parents on Central Park West and worked for his father in the garment district. Ron was nineteenth-century Chekhovian. To him, attending the ballet was like seeing Mickey Mantle and Willie Mays was to me. He would take a jet to London for a lunch date with Georgina Parkinson, a demi-soloist in the Royal Ballet. He had already taken three trips and, in my naive opinion, had more dollars in his backpack than I would put together in a lifetime. Ron wore Scali and Brioni suits, Denoyer ties, went to El Morocco, The Stork Club, French restaurants like Le Cirque and La Grenouille. He knew ballerinas: Allegra Kent, Jillana, Violette Verdy. He knew male dancers: Jacques D'Amboise. Edward Villella. We would frequently go to City Center and sit eighth row center. When I went only with Leslie, it was the last rows of the cavernous balcony. Ron even introduced me to George Balanchine and Lincoln Kirstein.

One December night in 1961, we went to the Copa. Matty "The Horse" Ianniello, the future crime boss of the Genovese crime family, his beloved wife, Beatrice May, Solomon, Hana, Morty Lefko (aka "The Colonel"), his wife, Leslie and me. That night Leslie was all legs, long and dangling and attracting attention. Hana Aroni was the most beautiful woman in the world that night. Carmine, the captain of the nightclub, a large handsome man wearing a black tux, was obviously familiar with both Matty Ianniello and Solomon. He seated us at a table out in front so that when the show started, the headline performer, Sammy Davis Jr., shook hands with both men. The comic who opened the show that night also came over to our table and said, "In my entire lifetime I've never seen such beautiful women with such ugly men." We all snickered a little and continued eating our Chinese. The Horse began talking about the recent World Series, when the Yankees beat the Cincinnati team in five games. It was the nineteenth championship in thirty-nine seasons for the Yankees, and Solomon and Matty were bragging about that as well as New York City. The women talked about their favorite films of the year. Matty's wife, The Colonel's, and Hana Aroni all loved *West Side Story* while Leslie's favorite was *Breakfast at Tiffany's*. Then The Horse said, "The best film of the year without a doubt was *Guns of Navarone*."

"No contest," Solomon Lepidus said.

All of us got along just fine until the women went to freshen up.

"I can't believe the stuff you put up with from that wife of yours, Matty," The Colonel said. "A tough guy like you."

Matty slowly drew his gun from its holster. Jammed the barrel deep into The Colonel's mouth. "What did you say?"

The Colonel pissed his pants.

To me it was funny. I knew Matty Ianniello could be dangerous, but I didn't think he was going to shoot The Colonel. And he didn't.

A year later in Solomon's office I slowly started to become less clueless.

Solomon wanted to connect me with Matty Ianniello. "Davey boy, The Horse has taken a liking to you. And by now, you know his reputation. He's known more for earning than for killing. And you know the way I feel about you. We're going to offer you something great." With that, Solomon waved to Joe Bruno, a felon recently released from the Otisville Correctional Facility and who was now Solomon's new head of security, to leave the office. He then called his secretary in. "Don't disturb us for at least an hour."

"Davey boy, I own several establishments that I want to transfer to you in name." Solomon pulled what seemed like a legal document from a desk drawer. "You sign these papers, and you'll be the owner of these here bars. As you can see, I'm throwing in The Wagon. I heard you took Leslie and Hana there. There are fifteen joints in all. They might be mostly gay joints, Davey boy, but it's a hundred dollars a month for you for each of them." Solomon pushed the papers under my nose."

"Sign here, Davey boy."

I hesitated.

"What's the matter, Davey boy? There's fifteen hundred a month for you for doin' nothing."

I thought of my father preaching to me, "You have an obligation to turn darkness into light, David. That's what men and women who do something good with their lives do. They turn darkness into light!"

"I can't do that, Solomon. My father's a cantor."

Everybody's Best Friend looked at me.

"That's okay, Davey boy. Let's go eat."

CHAPTER 4

I'm thinking that even as a kid I relished the real, the nitty-gritty of the New York life. Now, I'm wealthy, but I got here through hard work, headwork, dirty work. I still like and respect working men and women, but I wonder how "real" I am. How far behind have I left that fourteen-year-old boy who told his parents that private schools like Dalton and Horace Mann and Collegiate were not for him? I wanted to go to a public high school. "I don't want to be with just rich kids, Mom." My mother recognized that I would always find the super's kid to make friends with.

I wanted to go to Commerce, especially when I discovered that Lou Gehrig had gone there. That George Gershwin had gone there. Commerce High School had supers' kids, poor kids, over fifty percent of the student body were brown and black. My first day at Commerce, September 1951, a Negro boy took the seat next to me in homeroom. He was big headed and sober faced. He wore a starched white shirt, a striped red and gold tie, razor-creased chinos, a blue blazer with a plaid handkerchief in his breast pocket. I thought that strange. The good thing about it was that it made me take notice. Noah Weldon and I nodded at each other. It was chemistry or something. We immediately hit it off.

We weren't exactly in Commerce High School. We were on the third floor, which encompassed Lincoln Park Honor School. We were going to take a demanding academic curriculum. Be prepared for college. We would be burdened with state Regents Examinations. French or Spanish. Physics and chemistry, algebra and geometry and calculus. The boys and girls at Commerce, on the other hand, were taking shop, typing, general courses and didn't have to fret about Regents Exams or the pressures of preparing for college.

"I picked Commerce," I told Noah, "because I heard so much about its basketball program. Herman Wolf is one of the best coaches in the city. I heard this from guys like Dolph Schayes and Connie Simmons. I met them during my summers in the Catskills."

Noah had never heard of the Catskill Mountains. Dolph Schayes had played at NYU and was a superstar in the NBA; Connie Simmons was the center for the New York Knicks. I was always the kind of pretentious loser who threw out names. It's one of my long-term Broadway Dave flaws, but at fourteen, I just thought it was natural. Simmons and Schayes played at Klein's Hillside, the Catskill mountain hotel my parents and I stayed at summer after summer from the time I was six.

Noah Weldon was special. It wasn't anything that he said because Noah didn't talk very much. It was just something about his humble manner, his thoughtful brow, the smooth untroubled reserve that his voice exuded. Noah and I stayed together all that first morning. I began talking about basketball, and I knew the game. The basketball played at Klein's Hillside during the 1950s was not good or very good—it was great. George Mikan played there. Bob Cousy and Paul Arizin and Sonny Jamison and Paul Unruh and Eddie Younger and damn—the list of All Americans and professional stars was unending. By the middle of our first week, Noah and I were friends.

"Noah, I had to go to the bathroom. There was this guy there. He's on the basketball team. Must've been six foot eight. He asked me if I wanted a reefer. I said no. Noah, what's a reefer?"

Our homeroom teacher was also our French teacher, an owlish looking woman, fierce, with pursed lips, and a face that never opened. Mrs. Martin. She looked like every student's nightmare. Yet, like with most human beings, once you got to know her, Mrs. Martin was a very nice lady. With me, it didn't matter. Right after the first session of Mrs. Martin's French class, I walked out and switched to Spanish. Didn't help very much. I was always challenged when it came to foreign languages. On the other hand, with basketball, I knew every player in the NBA. I loved the game. Even back then I could gauge a player's value. Project his potential within minutes. Just knew. In the future, this gift changed my life. Noah and I didn't speak much about baskets. He was one of those boys you would never take for being gabby. We did speak about one girl that he had a crush on, her name was Joya Highsmith, and we spoke about Willie Mays and Mickey Mantle. Both of us agreed that these two major league rookies were going to be all-stars.

"I saw Willie's first home run off Warren Spahn, Noah. It went over the Polo Grounds' roof. I'm telling you, Willie Mays is going to be as great a ballplayer as Joe DiMaggio."

"And what's your prediction for Mantle?" Noah asked in a somewhat scoffing manner.

"Mantle has more power and speed than anyone I've ever seen. He makes Johnny Mize look like a singles hitter. He makes Sam Jethroe look as if he were Roy Campanella on the bases."

Mickey Mantle at nineteen could run to first in 3.1 seconds from the left side of the plate and in 3.6 seconds from the right. He could hit a baseball over five hundred feet. Ninety percent of New York City teenagers became Mickey Mantle worshippers in 1951. As for Willie, he was in a class by himself. The same league as Sugar Ray Robinson in boxing; Bob Cousy in basketball; Jim Brown in football. These men were the Prousts, the Tolstoys, and the Joyces—not just of 1951 but of all time. Now that I'm eighty years old with perspective, I know that to be truer than ever.

Noah and I talked about Mickey and Willie and Whitey Ford and Joe Ostrowski and Charlie Silvera and Yogi Berra and Paul Arizin and Sweetwater Clifton and Earl Lloyd and the two Bobbys—Wanzer and Davies. The two Bobby's were the backcourt for the Rochester Royals. Noah told me Bobby Wanzer had played for Commerce's bitter rival, Benjamin Franklin. Wanzer and Davies were Noah's favorite backcourt in the NBA. Mine were Cousy and Sharman.

"I admit Bobby Davies is great and Wanzer is clutch," I said, "but there's no one like Cousy. He's a magician. The greatest point guard in the history of the game." And Bob Cousy was just that until a player named "Oscar" came on court.

Late October of that year, I casually mentioned to Noah that I had seen some of the guys who were on our basketball team in the school auditorium. "One of them was the fellow who offered me a reefer. All of them are as huge as the players in the NBA and look stronger."

Noah shrugged his shoulders and began talking about *Gentleman's Agreement*, a book about anti-Semitism he had been reading and that he thought I would like. For some strange reason, he didn't talk much about basketball after that. He avoided the subject, and then, before I gave it much thought, it was basketball season.

The varsity was scrimmaging. Guys by the name of Williams and Gaines were our two stars. Both players had already been recruited by several colleges. Both were over six foot six, and both were jumpers. Noah was five foot eleven, perhaps a hundred-and-sixty pounds, probably less. He was preppy, delicate, pensive, like a Jewish boy from Riverside Drive. He was a good student, much better than me. I was getting mostly Bs, Noah was getting straight As. And then, one day, this best friend of mine for the last three months was in the school lunchroom with his girlfriend Joya and me sharing two of my mom's gigantic salmon, hard-boiled eggs with slices of tomato and chunks of chicken sandwiches, and I asked him, "Today at three, the basketball team is having its first pre-season game. Want to go watch them play?"

Noah quickly looked at Joya.

"I can't," he said.

I went alone. I walked into the Commerce gym with its old-school basketball court with the obligatory running track overhead where I jogged daily and spotted Noah. He was on the court. I was shocked. I watched him play for maybe ten minutes. No more. He wasn't just one of the players. Noah Weldon was the best player! This fifteen-year-old boy was a great basketball player. I had thought of Noah as more of a nerd than I wanted him to be. My parents loved Noah. Whenever he visited our home, after dinner, when my mother hugged and kissed him goodnight, she would tell him, "I wish I had a daughter for you."

Noah was hurt badly in his senior year. He blew out his knee. In those days, surgery wasn't what it is today. All but one of his forty-seven scholarship offers were taken away. The remaining one was at a small Catholic school. Of course, Noah took the offer. He played backcourt in college on one leg, but his transcendent quickness was gone. His speed was destroyed, so he played with craft and savvy. On one leg, he played Division One College ball, but his matchless game was gone and would never come back.

Christmas of 1956, Noah went with his college team to Owensboro, Kentucky to compete in the All-American City Basketball Tournament. He called me in the middle of the night.

"Dave, I'm sorry if I woke you. You're not going to believe what just happened. The University of Mississippi walked out of the tournament because I'm black. Tad Smith, the Ole Miss Athletics director, said, 'When we accepted the invitation to the tournament, it was with the understanding that there wouldn't be any Negroes in it.' My whole team went back to our motel. The guys refused to play without me."

Up until then, neither Noah nor I had known how sick the world could really get.

"You're not going to believe this either, Dave. When we were back in our hotel room, it must have been midnight, there's this knock on the door. Brendan McKinney was the only one of us who wasn't too scared to open it. When he did, there are these twelve white guys with crew cuts standing there. It was the Mississippi team we were supposed to play. They wanted to apologize in person. We invited them into our room. All of us got to know one another. I think that was great, don't you?"

And now I'm squinting at a photo in my collage. It's 1958. I'm in a tuxedo for the first time in my life. I'm best man at Noah Weldon's wedding. He's marrying Joya Highsmith, his high school sweetheart. Today Noah and Joya are over eighty years old and still in love.

CHAPTER 5

Those days working for the *Mirror* and living in my bachelor pad on 56th Street, life was full. And I was sleeping with Leslie Kore, when she had the time.

Most of the time, she didn't. Leslie was always juggling men, always hunting for a super-rich husband. I knew the last guy Leslie Kore wanted to marry was a $48-a-week copyboy. In those days, I read voraciously and attempted to write though I didn't have much to say. I had an active social life, going out, having parties. Once I organized a paint party with my friends. We painted the walls in my West 56th Street apartment. I can still see the vibrant reds, blues, yellows, and purples on those walls.

My friends were great. We had our own rat pack back then. Howie Puris was dating a woman twice his age. "What can I tell ya? Rose knows everything that I'd want a woman to know." Al Kasha, who would win a couple of Oscars as a songwriter for *The Towering Inferno* and *The Poseidon Adventure*. Even Phil Spector came over once in a while. Phil would go on and on about this thing he had been working on, his "Wall of Sound" technique, which he liked to say was his Wagnerian approach to rock 'n' roll. At that time, he didn't seem bizarre or crazy—just earnest and onto something big.

Those were exciting times, but I was doing something most guys weren't. I was fantasizing about one day becoming a serious novelist. I never wanted to be a Random House CEO like Bennett Cerf or Robert Gottlieb, the future president of Knopf. I never was a dedicated aesthete, though, as I said, I read everything, and I loved the ballet almost as much as Ron Nevins. I was bringing women—by which I mean long-legged dancers—to my 56th Street pad on a regular basis. We'd listen to Frank and Nina Simone and Ray Charles, and it worked for a while. And then I started to see Leslie Kore on a more serious basis. Leslie and I were open about seeing other people. In fact, we made a bet whenever we went to a single's bar.

"I'll wager you, David, that I pick up six men before you get the phone number of one woman."

Leslie always won, but in those carefree days, it didn't really matter.

I was working for the *New York Daily Mirror*, I was twenty-four, and I was loving my life. And then Leslie began to bust my chops that I needed to make money. I wimped out and quit the *Mirror*, the job I loved. I telephoned my friend Ron Nevins.

"Don't worry, Broadway. I'll speak to my father. I'll get him to start you off at two hundred dollars a week. We can go to Le Cirque for lunch. Go to the ballet every night."

When I told Leslie, she started to take me seriously. The sex that night wasn't half as good. Why didn't that tip me off to the mistake I'd made?

When I walked into the office of Mr. Nevins, he said, "Sit down, David. Make yourself comfortable. I've known you a long time, and I know you'll hate it down here in the garment center. In good conscience, I can't do this to you."

A return to the Public Assistance job looked right around the corner.

As for Leslie Kore, from "Get a real job . . ." to "Take a walk . . ." took less than a month.

Within six months, Leslie, with her looks and a preternaturally high 165 I.Q., was engaged to a dashing Harvard man, an investment banker. What was I doing? Pounding my head against my red, blue, yellow, and purple walls. And not only because of losing Leslie, but also because I had walked away from the *Mirror*. Of course, I'd loved the fabulous parties I covered and the beautiful women I met. But there was more to it. I loved being in a newsroom, being part of the unfolding investigative reporting, the shouting of the editors, columnists like Suzy, as much involved with the big stories as the hard boiled, big-bellied, black coffee, crossword puzzle newspaper lifers, the entire paper clamoring and buzzing, cub reporters, grizzled veterans, copyboys, rotary phones that never stopped ringing, copy desk white-haired antiques like Phil McGee scribbling succinct captions, asking me, "Hey kid! What do you think of this one?"

I quit that fantasy job because of Leslie's Kore's ultimatum: "Your salary is $48 a week. Get real, David. You must make money."

I paid mightily for that mistake. And I would pay more yet.

It was 1962, and I was working in Public Assistance, this time, on 126th Street off Park. It was the same job, but I wasn't the same, fresh-faced innocent I'd been in 1958. At twenty-one, fresh out of college, when being a Social Investigator was my first job, I was crazy to bring light into the world, as my father said. I looked forward each day to all the good I wanted to do. Five years later, so much jism had been knocked out of me, I could hardly remember my unstained self's enthusiasm for the work.

I was enthusiastic about *The Tutor*, the novel I'd written. I phoned John Farrar, one of the three head honchos at Farrar, Straus and Giroux. FSG was one of the most prestigious publishing houses in the country. It was like calling Elia Kazan cold and trying to convince him that you're the next Brando. Miraculously, I got Mr. Farrar on the phone and told him about my novel.

"Young man," he said, "my wife and I are leaving the city for our country house in one hour, and it just so happens that I haven't much to read this weekend. If you can be down here . . . "

I raced out of the Welfare Department!

On Monday morning at 7:15 A.M. John Farrar called me. "Young man, in all my years in publishing, this is the most special novel I've read by an unpublished novelist. What I would like to do is assign an editor to you. Mrs. Zasky is in Europe right now, but I'm going to fly her into New York when she finishes up the project she's working on, and, if you are willing, have her work with you. Mrs. Zasky is the most suitable editor for your novel that I know of."

Eight months later, Mr. Farrar phoned. "I didn't realize that we were publishing three iconoclastic novels this year. I can't justify a fourth."

All of this took place immediately after Leslie left me for dead. I was still almost a hormone-flooded teenager. Still with dreams, the artless idealism of youth. And so was much of our society, in a manner of speaking. Doubly so in the world of New York publishing. In the sixties, words meant something. Literature, novelists, men of letters were relevant. People were reading. We—some of us at least—had our beaks in dense books, communicating with deep, angry roars, introspecting, studying philosophers, poets, Shakespeare. We had the naiveté to believe that we could help change the world. Yes, it was a different world, and, yes, I thought that I was a part of it. And, yes, I believed I had real value.

I wanted to be a novelist. When that telephone call from John Farrar came in, I didn't write again for two years. I coughed up *The Baseball Rating Handbook* and a basketball book. But I didn't write *write*. I was dead inside. I was fragile. We're all so fragile. Writing a book meant something. Being published was like touching God. With *The Tutor* I was trying to do something with dignity, something sublime. Something that involved all the best of me. A novelist was as good as the ladder he tried to climb and the challenges he undertook. The risks he took on his slippery trapeze. Once he compromised and didn't make his reader move in the direction of an uncorrupted star, forget about it. It was time for Hollywood. It was time for handicapping.

CHAPTER 6

O ne year ago, I learned that Jessica Strauss had died. I hadn't seen Jessica in more than fifty-five years, but I drove into the city to attend the memorial service. I took a seat in the last row at the chapel and listened to her friends and family tell their stories. Afterward, I couldn't bring myself to go back to Westchester. Instead, I went to my penthouse. I couldn't stop myself from thinking. Of what could have been. Of what went wrong. Of what a lowlife I'd been for so much of my life. Outside of a few years, until I was sixty-two and met Elizabeth Dunn, I'd lived a life dedicated to selfishness in everything that really counted. I paced my rooftop all night thinking about Jessica Strauss. How I almost cost Jessica her life when we were so perfectly young.

Jessica Strauss came into my life in 1963. She was twenty-two. I was twenty-six. Leslie Kore had married that Harvard banker and been out of my life for almost two years. Soon Jessica and I became seriously involved. I proposed. She accepted. I arranged for our engagement party to be held at Danny's Hideaway, one of the ultra-in places back in the day. Jessica deserved a cool party. She was the best person I had ever known. Kind, trusting, real.

"I might be working for the Welfare Department, Jess, but I still have some influential contacts at the *Mirror*."

"As long as we're together, it doesn't matter to me where we have our engagement party or if we have a party at all. It just doesn't matter. What matters is that we're together. That's what makes me happy."

We went to Yankee games. On weekends to L'Entre-Deux, a swank, private club in the basement of the Gotham Hotel on 55th Street between Fifth and Sixth Avenues frequented primarily by suave European trash. We'd dance to The Twist till one in the morning, then we'd go for a nightcap at Jimmy Wynn's Harwyn Club or to the Eden Roc and dance some more. We always finished off our Saturday nights at the Brasserie on 53rd and Park, where the main room's hostess,

Marie, would direct us to the table where my friends were. Guys like the promoter, Stickers.

"I'm putting together this idea I have to present Frank Sinatra at Carnegie Hall. Tomorrow, I'm meeting Solomon for brunch at Barney Greengrass. I hope Solomon's in a good mood. I'm going to ask him for the money to do the concert."

I had many friends back in those days. Sometimes creeps like Elizabeth Taylor's friend, Dennis Stein, would join us.

"What are you doing, Dave?"

"I'm trying to write."

"How's your penmanship?"

Jessica loved going to the Bronx Zoo, talking to me about having our children.

"We're going to have five, David," she'd say. Jessica was sure of that.

Then, out of nowhere, Leslie Kore telephoned.

"I have a problem. I must see you."

The problem was Leslie's Harvard man had found her in bed with another man. The way Leslie spoke about her Harvard man made him sound, well, worse than me.

I met Leslie for a cocktail. We ended up at my place, a neat one-bedroom apartment in a redbricked building near the two great museums on upper Fifth Avenue. Jessica and I both loved exploring those museums. For the next six months, I was a tennis ball. Back 'n' forth. It was crazy, it was beyond difficult, it was impossible.

My mom said it's only a matter of time before my eyes would open. My father said, "I knew when you stopped going to synagogue that you would end up like this." I spoke to Noah Weldon. "David, it's simple. The girl you like holding hands with. The one you feel is your best friend. That's the one to marry."

Noah's wife, Joya, said, "Damn, Lazar! You're a fool! Jessica's a great girl, and Leslie, well . . . she's Leslie . . . "

Six months later, Leslie and I were caught at the Hotel Wellington by Leslie's husband, his uncle, and a detective. The three of them managed to force their way into our hotel room, where Leslie and I were clinging to each other under Wellington sheets. We were guilty, more than guilty. We were fucked.

"You're a whore!" Leslie's Harvard man kept shouting at her.

Harvard's uncle kept saying, "Let's everyone just settle down."

The detective looked like Dick Cheney. He was taking Polaroids, salivating, ogling Leslie, and Leslie was a treat to ogle.

"David, it's time you break off your ridiculous engagement," Leslie said in a controlled tone. "We must get married when this skirmish is over." She shook her head and bare shoulders and the rest of her flawlessness and tossed the Wellington sheets.

"This is the last look at a perfect ten that you'll ever get!" she told Harvard.

Her husband was speechless. So was I. Marry Leslie? It was Jessica I loved. This Leslie wasn't close to the same woman who recited to me the sonnets of the Bard, adored Othello, was passionate about the writings of Jean Rhys. Leslie was forced to leave Cornell because her parents ganged up on her. Insisted she marry a trust-fund heir. Her 165 I.Q.? It didn't matter. Her ambition to be a surgeon? Irrelevant.

And I also kept thinking, "What makes me the a-hole I am?"

Even then I recognized it.

"I would like it very much if one of you gentlemen poured me a glass of Dom Perignon," Leslie said. Dick Cheney rushed over and started pouring. I tried to cover Leslie up.

She flung off the sheets, and shrieked, "Let my husband get a good look! It's the last one he'll ever get of me!"

Not long after, I walked down a hospital corridor to see Jessica. Jessica's mother and father were guarding the door. I took a deep breath.

"Excuse me," I said.

"We don't want you to go into our daughter's room," Mrs. Strauss said. "You've already caused enough damage, David."

"Please, I just want to see Jess. Please let me get by."

Jessica's father, a large burly man who worked at the Brooklyn Navy Yard, stiffened. "You're not getting in there!"

"Mr. Strauss, I feel terrible about what's happened. I love your daughter."

Jessica's parents looked at me as if I were crazy.

Something inside me took over. I pushed my way through Mr. and Mrs. Strauss. Pale, her wrists bandaged, her eyes bloodshot, Jessica looked small, and Jessica wasn't a small girl. She was long legs, modest bust, and kindly smiles. She had apple-cheeks and thick, jet-black hair, the face of an ingénue, wholesome enough to be plastered on the cover of *Seventeen*.

Wincing, Jessica propped herself up on the bed. Tears began to trickle down her cheeks. "You know I love you, David. Leslie doesn't. She's a bad person." Jessica's eyes opened wide. "Leslie's not a good person, David. She has a spell over you. She'll make you unhappy."

I didn't hear a word. Not in the way you need to hear words. You have to be open to hear words. To listen. To take heed.

"I'm sorry, Jess," I said softly. I loved Jessica. She made me feel as if I were a good person. One night in a Brooklyn restaurant, Jess stood up at a gathering of several friends of mine to celebrate my first book being published. These friends had been teasing me for slurping my onion soup.

"Stop picking on David! You should all be ashamed of yourselves! David is a genius." Jessica was as uncomplicated as the 1950s. A lovely young woman with a grab bag of good intentions.

"I can't fight Leslie, David. She knows everything there is to know about sex. I know nothing but that I love you."

Perhaps my unbridled lust for Leslie Kore was the biggest shortcoming of my life. I always had a good feeling whenever Jessica and I were together. The kind of feeling that you can't buy.

I stopped pacing my rooftop terrace, walked inside the penthouse, and grabbed a snapshot of Jessica that I had peeled from one of my collages. I sat in front of the fireplace and looked at Jessica standing next to me and laughing. It seemed more like now than yesteryear. At eight in the morning, I called Elizabeth and started to enumerate the kind of dirtbag I was.

"I don't know that person. He sounds awful," she said.

Sweet-faced Jessica is gone. I destroyed what we had shared. We didn't remain friends. I never saw Jessica in all the decades that have passed. She disappeared. I'm forcing myself to believe that Jessica Strauss had a decent life, a husband who loved her before her gentle soul left this earth. But if she did, it was no thanks to me.

CHAPTER 7

I married Leslie Kore in 1965 when both of us were in our late twenties. We got hitched at city hall. It wasn't romantic or a marriage made in clueless heaven, more like the other place. During the five years I was married to Leslie, she complained I didn't make enough money, she howled about my gambling, she was a shrew. But, she had good cause for the way she was. There's no photograph in my collages for things that happened in those days, understandably, but I remember them clearly.

In 1966 Leslie was pregnant. I was working for the Welfare Department, taking home in the neighborhood of two hundred dollars a week. I was desperate to make more money. That doesn't excuse my degenerate gambling or any of the things that I allowed to happen. I didn't know there was such a thing as winning, much less how to win at something as arcane as handicapping college basketball. I was the screw-up. The one who got into trouble with outlaws.

I owed $2,800 to Abe Gold, an old-school Jewish bookmaker, a veteran of the Warsaw Ghetto, a man whose smile could freeze the blood in your veins. He had his office in his home in Hastings-on-Hudson and had planted more than a few people who did not pay him under his acres of lawn. Abe Gold sent two uglies over to my home to collect.

At one in the morning, I was getting ready to take a bath, and Leslie was in our one bedroom at the Regency Towers, which sounded fancy, but we were renting in the sub-basement. Our rent and sticks of furnishing were appropriate for a loser like me. When I heard the knock on the door, I knew who it was. I took a deep breath. I had to open the door. No good in not doing so. The uglies on the other side would kick the door down if I didn't. That's how far it had gone with Abe Gold. He had sent more than three serious ultimatums, and I had stalled and stalled for months. I told Leslie, "Please stay in the bedroom." She didn't. I opened the door.

The two uglies were not in a good mood. The smaller one was by no means little, the kind of Neanderthal with no body fat, who could hold his own with a professional fighter. He carried a baseball bat. The bigger one didn't have to. Both stared at Leslie. She was in her second month, but her see-through nightgown showed a perfect body. The two uglies started to come on to her. Leslie cursed them out. She threatened to call the police. The ugly with the baseball bat took his cigarette from his mouth and put it out on Leslie's arm. The huge ugly grabbed her by the hair and slammed her against the brick wall.

I had never seen Leslie look as frightened as she did then. In all the years I had known her, I had never once seen Leslie out of control, vulnerable. She was always in charge, adamant in every assertion. Always in command, smug. Now she was terrified. To me this enhanced her beauty. The fear on her face, that wilted regality, her new, more fragile look, it did something to me. It made me fall in love, in love with Leslie Kore, maybe for the very first time. Wanting not only to sleep with her but to cherish her; not only to flaunt her but to protect her. And in that instant, I hurled myself at the two uglies.

The six-feet-five and two-hundred-sixty-pound monster started to work me over. The smaller one joined in with his Louisville Slugger. Before they left, the uglies gave me two cents worth of advice. The Slugger said, "We're letting you off lightly this time. Mr. Gold likes you because you're Jewish."

The monster said, "If I were you, Yid, I would take seriously what my partner is capable of doing. He doesn't go to Temple every week. Neither does Mr. Gold."

I ended up at Lenox Hill Hospital with a fractured jaw and one of my arms in a cast. The following day when Leslie and I returned to the Towers, Leslie poured herself a stiff drink. She didn't say very much. I telephoned Solomon Lepidus. He was somewhere in San Juan, Puerto Rico. I couldn't reach him. I telephoned my best friend, Ron Nevins. "Ron, you have to help me! I'm in a lot of trouble! I'm desperate!" Ron, as always, came through.

The most incredible part of all of this was not that I survived the beating. It was that Leslie didn't leave me right then and there. She and I had sex that night, even though I could hardly breathe. She remained at my side. She had Heather, our baby girl.

Heather was our beaming baby girl. At six weeks she died of SIDS. Leslie didn't lose her grip. Within two months of Heather's death, Leslie started screaming, "I want a baby! I must have a child!" I wasn't insensitive, I just knew with our circumstances it was impossible. Leslie obviously was suffering greatly from the loss of Heather. Her need to replace Heather was not only valid, a large part of me thought the same, yet, I forced myself to exclaim that we couldn't afford a baby. She soon straightened her shoulders, made herself as beautiful as she could. Approaching thirty, she was no longer perfect, yet she went out on "go-sees" way before I stopped wiping Heather tears from my red eyes. Nothing we had experienced in all our years together came close to losing Heather.

Leslie stayed five years through my begging: banks, finance companies, friends, and relatives. Begging! Begging! "I need your help . . ." Leslie stayed. Leslie stayed and stayed . . . Leslie finally had had enough. Enough of my trying to write the Great American Novel. Enough of my views on American racism. Enough of my civil-service employments. Enough of my betting on baseball games, basketball games, football games. Betting . . . Betting . . . Betting! Losing and losing! More losing! More gambling. More and more Leslie shrieking, "Get a real job! You gambler! You gambler!!!"

Leslie was not that bad. She was the woman I loved, intermittently, for seventeen years. And during those seventeen years, no man I've ever known, read about in novels, or viewed on the big screen, ever enjoyed fucking a woman more. As much as I may want to blame Leslie Kore, I plainly see what kind of bottom-line asshole I was.

CHAPTER 8

Everything always came down to money. Leslie swept the broom, and I had to move in with my parents. A thirty-three-year-old loser moving back into his "boy's room." In those days, I couldn't afford a Hershey bar. My mother's health was deteriorating. Seeing her in pain daily was anguish. Despite insulin injections, a heart ailment, arthritic spine, palpitations, oxygen mask, an inability to transport herself without her walker, in and out of ICUs, my mom kept going. Teaching, doing her charity work while beached like that proverbial whale on her bed, Mom kept making a cheerful face. My dad clung to what had been, constantly telling himself and me, "Your mother is going to be okay. She's taking her medications. Going for rehab. The doctors are the best ones that I could find. They're helping. Tomorrow my Pearl will be herself again." And then, invariably, he would pray. I saw the self-deception in this kind of sophistry, the long-term self-denial. The false hopes.

I told myself, Leslie was gone forever. I stopped mourning the past. I'm not sure if I condemned myself for selfishness or lauded myself for thinking with clarity. Was it a strength of mine or something so much less that turned on the I'll Show Her mode for me? Or was it just me trying to look after Me! Me! Me!? At thirty-three, I began focusing on finding a new life. I kept trying to change my circumstances. "I'll show Leslie," and that meant trying to prepare myself to make a living. I studied all sorts of sports—baseball, football, professional basketball— without seeing how I could make a business of betting on any of them. And then I discovered a flaw in the predications bookies were making for the Vegas line of college basketball. I would calculate my numbers, and I found that out of the 4000 games played in a season, the Las Vegas line has at least 150 games four points or more off from my number. This meant something. It meant everything. Every half-a-point in my favor could mean dollars to me. Damn, every half-a-point (in my opinion) that Vegas was mistaken on was as if I was being resurrected with fresh air. Fresh air to a dying man. Keep breathing! Each half-a-point meant I could breathe. Four points from the Vegas line meant a life! Do you understand what I'm saying? I believed, as strongly as some believe in God, that I had found a way to make a living . . . I was always tinkering with numbers and developing power ratings to compete against the point spread. In other sports, no luck. Now I was convinced that I could compete against the Vegas line. In my opinion, they were wrong on at least 150 games out of the 4,000 they placed a point spread on from my line. My line was, granted, only mine, but I was confident that it was correct. Yes, that was just my opinion, but I was ultra-sophisticated when it came to basketball. A.S. Barnes had already published my analytics handbook, rating every player and every team in the history of the game. I was far from a novice.

It was difficult to keep up with studying handicapping while watching my mother die. My absorption in handicapping stole my generosity, my devotion. For the next two years, learning handicapping was my life. I struggled to balance my evolving handicapping skill with living with my dying mother. Was it weakness or strength on my part, or just plain necessity, that I continued to live like that as well as trudge to the Welfare Department five days a week? Without a dollar in my pocket, there was no opportunity to feel, "Fuck you, world! I'm free!" I continued to live in my parent's home as an adult male without many choices, a man who felt sorrier for himself than for his mother and father.

I kept studying, researching, and learning, discovering the things I needed to see green dollars, the things that I hoped would set me free, but never for a minute did I believe that anything I was doing was going to change my life. I wasn't a businessman with a bottom line investment. Or an accountant, who knows that one step leads to another. I was flying on instinct and hope, as stupid as I had always been, only this time I could look forward to possibility rather than be squashed by Leslie's "get a real job" nine-to-five domesticity.

While living in the boy's room, I tucked away $250 a nickel, a dime, or a dollar at a time. I started handicapping with a $25 wager. By the end of my first college basketball season, I had a profit of $4,300. The next hoop season, I started with $2,500, and I made $42,000. That's when I moved out of my parents' home. The third year that I handicapped, I made $109,000 and that's when my friend Morty Lefko, The Colonel—as good a peddler and promoter as there ever was—started telling the world that he knew a college basketball handicapper who was making money. Action guys started coming out of the woodwork, just as if I were a smooth-talking hedge fund hustler or a partner at Goldman Sachs.

To my father's religion, I had a deaf ear. In other matters, I listened to him.

"David," he would thunder after he finished his morning scales. (Dad never stopped preparing, demanding more and more from his voice.) "David! Failing to prepare is preparing to fail!"

I would work through the night, bleary-eyed, until four, five in the morning, studying who chewed gum. Who didn't. Everything that might influence a game. Things that were real, farfetched, one in a million, I wrote it all in my loose-leaf binder that I named my "Holy Book." I wrote my father's words in bold letters on the front cover.

"Failing to prepare is preparing to fail."

Money soon became the drug that kept me going. Winning games! Profit! More money! Counting $100 bills as if they were Tootsie Roll wrappers, one after the other. It took me hours to count those Franklins. Eventually, I learned from Nathan Rubin, how to count these freshly minted bills by rifling them close to my ear and listening for the click.

Once I began to handicap college basketball, my soul became money. Writing novels became secondary. Money was sacrosanct. Stuffing wads of bills into designated packages. Rubber-banding them as if I were a Columbian drug dealer. Placing these stacks of bills into safe deposit boxes at neighborhood banks. Soon I learned about the Cayman Islands and other sly places in the world that gave you a serial number, a safe harbor, a strong box.

I'm looking at my collages and thinking how I was never turned on by legitimate business. I loved writing. Not that I ever made any real money at it. I spot the book jacket of the bestseller I wrote in 1981, based on my life, but even that book didn't earn what I'd make in four weeks of handicapping. (When gambling beats art, something is certainly fucked up in this world.) I never wanted to own a company. Solomon Lepidus did. He was a man of many parts. Solomon would arrange for the Carnegie Deli to deliver three hundred turkey dinners to homeless people every year. I loved the guy. He became the biggest investor in my handicapping ventures. Unfortunately, he was a compulsive gambler. He was once so flush that he tried to buy the New York Yankees. For twenty-five years, the two of us shared laughs. Then things changed. There were only sixteen people at his memorial service, for a man who at one time could've run for mayor and won in a landslide. People like people on top. We're all messed up in so many ways. Many are decent for a long while, but then, one day, even they have to look in the mirror.

That's what I'm doing.

During those hard years living with my parents, I was without a clue as to how I was going to make it. I'm glad I had Solomon Lepidus as a friend. He would tell me the biggest mistake is overthinking the past and underthinking the future. Back then it sounded like gibberish, but now I understand what he meant. Don't dwell, move forward is part of it, but more than that, he meant find a purpose, go to work, do something with the time you have. Before you catch your breath, it's all over.

This champion amongst men, Solomon Lepidus, introduced me to celebrities, politicians, federal and state judges, and everyone else who came into his steakhouse. Many times, I had dinner with "The prime minister"—Frank Costello, the American mafia gangster and crime boss. Once I was at the restaurant when Solomon was at another table having drinks with Matty The Horse Ianniello. I remember that night because Solomon had tears in his eyes. He had been told that Frank Costello had died.

Everyone's best friend, Solomon Lepidus, was larger than his criminal lifestyle. Four years after the prime minister died, Solomon was at his restaurant with president Jimmy Carter and Leon Charney, an authority on the Middle East. They were discussing and planning the early stages of the Camp David accords. My best friend was a whole lot more than lifestyle. I'm the kind of male who was immersed in gambling and problematic relationships. Solomon Lepidus was always immersed in much larger issues.

And he was always making a point.

"Davey boy, when you shake somebody's hand and give your word, you've got to honor it—or else! And Davey boy, a word to the wise, never admitting to a lie is necessary for a whole lot of pants as well as skirts. Catch what I'm sayin'?"

Nathan Rubin is in my collage, as well he should be. Not only was he one of my limited partners, he was more than that. Month after month, at my studio apartment or his Park Avenue triplex, he mentored me in handicapping college basketball. He talked; I listened.

Rubin started out an orphan. When I knew him, he was seventy-six, cold, white-haired, dapper, and had done just about everything there was to do. He had accumulated dollars to fulfill the American greed dream, but in Rubin's veins was an insatiable need for more. Always more dollars.

Nathan Rubin worked with Meyer Lansky, the mob's accountant, and, back in the day, came up with scamming race tracks by past posting through wire services. Past posting means placing a bet after the game or race has started. The dynamics have changed. I have an edge and I take advantage of it (past post). It can get you killed. But beyond tampering with wire services and past posting, Rubin was the king of the card counters. By the time he was real cold, he had already been banned from casinos from Las Vegas to Monte Carlo, so he started hiring and tutoring young men who had attended MIT, Harvard, Princeton—people like John Talbot and Tobias Roth—how to count cards to improve their odds at winning blackjack. When Las Vegas went to two decks for blackjack, Nathan Rubin still figured out ways for his people to gain an edge.

"Davey Boy," Solomon Lepidus told me more than once. "There's no one like Nathan Rubin. He's the best card player and proposition man in the gambling world, and let me warn you right now, Davey Boy, he'll screw you out of your first dollar and your last."

Solomon and Rubin were rivals, friends, great enemies, but Rubin considered Solomon a sucker. In all the years I knew them, not once did Solomon ever win a proposition bet from Nathan Rubin.

Nathan Rubin would drill into me day by day, hour after hour, what to look for in handicapping college basketball: senior backcourts, conservative game plans, no playground players, revenge games. A team that doesn't turn the ball over. A fan base that goes crazy.

"Everyone's a sucker, Sonny. That's the main thing to know. In New York, suckers like to bet the games played at the Garden. They'd rather bet on St. John's against Syracuse or Georgetown than Miami of Ohio against Central Michigan or Kent State against Bowling Green. That's wrong thinking, Sonny. You should always look for the conferences that people don't have exposure to. You want an example? Well, here's one. The Mid-American Conference. The players are three stars, sometimes two. No five-star McDonald's All-Americans playin' for Bowling Green or Toledo or Eastern Michigan. Sixteen schools in the Mid-American. You should study and learn as much as you can about both the east and west divisions. That's a lot of schools and games without much exposure, and even more importantly, these kinds of teams do not have the athletes to run up scores that go into the eighties or the nineties. These colleges are lucky if they reach sixty-five or seventy points in a game. And that's what you want. You want scores that are as low as possible. Rather than Duke or North Carolina or Kentucky or Kansas that score in the nineties and win by twenty, you want teams that score in the sixties and seventies and win by five. You grab the short in those games, Sonny. Take your seven, eight, nine, or eleven points, and you stick with the short for a lifetime. You can't go wrong. Get what I'm sayin', Sonny? You want great coaches with mediocre players. Coaches who make sure that their players know the fundamentals. Play the game basket to basket. Don't turn the ball over. That's why you always want a junior or senior backcourt. Give me a four-year senior over a freshman hotshot every time. And let me tell you something else. You find a wide-bodied, big assed, six-five center who takes up space, has a touch, is hungry to rebound and who anchors his team, and you're getting a whole lot more value than some seven-foot drink of water who's coming out of high school with the reputation of being the next Wilt or Jabbar or Russell.

"There might not be any bandboxes left, Sonny, but the students attending the games make a large difference. Home courts, Sonny. Home courts with points in a 'revenge game' and you got a live short. Always look to take the points, Sonny."

Nathan Rubin was always mentoring me. Sometimes trying to steal from me but all the time fascinating me. Several times, when I was at his Park Avenue triplex, he would be on the phone, negotiating a deal that I couldn't even dream of doing. In the middle of one those negotiations, with his britches off, his spindly legs bare, his knee socks and candy-striped boxer shorts all there was between him and embarrassment, Margaret, his housekeeper, walked into the room.

Rubin took the telephone from his ear.

"Margaret, how much did you pay for the Mop & Glo, the Mr. Clean, and that can of Ajax? Do you have receipts?"

Rubin studied the receipts.

"That's way too much money!" he screeched. "I told you, Margaret, don't shop at Gracious Home! You should have gone to that bodega on 1st Avenue. They're at least ten percent cheaper!"

He then stamped his feet on the parquet floor and glared at his housekeeper.

"Margaret, you know I'm going to have to take the $1.72 difference out of your paycheck."

Then Nathan Rubin calmly returned to his phone call.

He lived in high society as well as the low. He was the CEO of Metropolitan Cable, owned a chain of funeral parlors, a fleet of sanitation trucks. I think he was connected to The Horse in his DEUCE prostitution business. It's possible that Solomon was, too. During the early seventies, Solomon even offered me a piece of The Peppermint, as sleazy a bar as Violette Leduc could ever have conceived. Rubin also owned parking lots, which decades later were converted into seventy-story office towers. He had his port-wine-stained forearms in much more stuff. This cantor's son was traumatized at the age of eight when he accidently murdered a pigeon with a clothes hanger in Strauss Park. Even more traumatized at the age of eleven, when a window washer lost his footing and splattered in front of me, but ironically, instead of feeling horrified by Nathan Rubin and Solomon Lepidus, I remained enamored with them for far too long.

Though they were both deceased by the time I met Elizabeth, she has told me more than once that I should stop idealizing them.

CHAPTER 9

From the beginning with Debbie Turner, whom I met in my second stint at Welfare, it was as if I had found just what I was looking for after Leslie: the closeness, the true friendship, the feeling that every minute not shared was a minute not worth living. Every weekday morning, I woke up in a rush to brush my teeth, splash my face with cold water, slap on some deodorant, hurry uptown so that before the day started, the case histories and pendings began to pile up on my desk, the drug addicts started depressing me, the infirmed started to take their toll so that I would have those ten to fifteen perfect minutes with Debbie Turner. She was as much a pick-me-up as a five-hundred-foot homerun by Mickey Mantle had been during my teenage years. From 7:45 A.M. to 8:00 A.M., it was Debbie Turner time. Deb was always hitting one out of the park and in those days, months, and for those first two or three years, she was—in capital letters—MY HAPPINESS PILL. I breathed her in. Gulped her down. Listened to her cackle. Gazed at her open face. Just Debbie saying "hi" to me was a joy.

Debbie Turner was a radical change of pace from everything else in my life. As far away from my tribulations as Central Park in June is from Central Park in January. Debbie Turner was needed.

"Debbie, here's all you've got to know about my marriage to Leslie: she and I went down to City Hall. We got hitched. We left the building. Leslie wanted Japanese. I wanted Chinese. We got into a fight. Leslie got in one cab. I got into another. We didn't see each other for two weeks. That was as close as we ever got to marital bliss."

Debbie's supervisor, Boris Tuttle, your typical civil servant broke in. "I hate interrupting your conversation with Mr. Lazar, Ms. Turner, but one of your pendings is in in-take and needs your immediate attention."

"I'll walk with you, Debbie."

I didn't spell it out to Deb, but the reason I accompanied her wasn't only that I wanted to be with her. The in-take section was in the basement, an isolated area where drug addicts out of Rikers prison were hanging out. Several violent incidents had taken place there that month.

"You must understand, Debbie," I said. "Pending cases are impossibly difficult. Some people who apply for assistance are desperate. Don't waste time asking recipients a lot of policy questions. Just find out how you can help. And help."

"Oh, my God!" Debbie gasped. I turned around. Twenty feet from us was a woman lying on the floor, having a seizure. Several clients were milling around her and staring. Two senior caseworkers were standing there chatting. Not doing a damned thing. I raced over. Grabbed my wallet out of my back pocket. Shoved it into the woman's mouth. When she continued having difficulty with her breathing, I started to give her mouth-to-mouth. Didn't know exactly what else to do. I conjectured it was either an epileptic seizure or a heart attack. I guessed an epileptic convulsion.

Thirty minutes later, Debbie said, "That was amazing, David! You were fantastic! I've never seen anyone do anything like that before!" Debbie gazed at me. I never forgot her gaga look.

When I was with Debbie, I was happy. What made me sad was her leaving the office on Friday afternoons. Those long weekends when I wouldn't see her. Remembering those gaga moments until the following Monday.

How stupid I was. I felt that our Mondays through Fridays would never end. We'd go for Chinese on 86th Street and Lexington.

"Here's a story on Solomon Lepidus, Debbie. This happened the first time we had dinner together. He said, 'Davey Boy, you're always carrying a book.'"

That one was a philosophy book with in-depth looks at Heidegger, Nietzsche, Beckett, Camus, Kierkegaard, and others I revered. "Solomon grabbed the book from my hand, read the jacket cover, looked up. 'You think these guys can teach you something that I can't?' I just stared at him, Debbie. What could I say?"

We would thrill each other just by being together—no touching, no nothing, just talking. Debbie would talk effusively about her fiancé, Michael Edison. "Michael and I spent the weekend at his married sister's house. We read, discussed the books we were reading, and I did a *New York Times* crossword puzzle while Michael read the Science section. We did a little cooking and after dinner, Michael discussed with his sister their plans for their annual summer getaway. You know what I loved the most during the entire weekend? Getting on the floor and playing with Alice's children."

Once Debbie started talking, she couldn't be stopped. For me it was relaxing, something about her nasal voice, her conversations, invariably put me close to sleep. What awakened me was when I looked across the table, and my eyes traveled to Debbie's bosom.

Three years later, I attended her wedding on her parents' front lawn in Bethesda, Maryland. She and Michael moved out of New York. Nine months later, she called me.

"I can't live with Michael any longer. I think of you all the time."

Debbie Turner moved in with me. I remember our first kiss as if it was yesterday. It took place on my rooftop. We were no longer just friends.

Soon after, what we shared began to disappear, not all at once, of course, but a scintilla at a time. How sad when that happens. I began to feel more alone than I had before it all had happened. I felt as if I would have been better off if it had never happened. Debbie Turner was my happiness pill, but once Debbie's friends started to show up in New York, those women from Bethesda and Silver Spring and all those other hamlets with white picket fences and families of brats, that's when I lost it. Debbie would plan for baby showers and gossip with her friends about girl–boy relationships for hours at a time. That was her life. It wasn't mine. Her friends would want to go on vacation with us. In the middle of winter, I would be freezing my nuts off out on my rooftop with my nine phones, getting lines and making bets.

"Debbie, I can't take a vacation. I'm working. You think I'm going to leave the city to go on some freakin' ski trip in Aspen?"

I wanted to work. When you go to war, you don't take a vacation.

And then one day, Debbie said, "I don't deserve the way you're treating me, David. I've acted in good faith, but I can no longer take the way you are. It's not that you're difficult. I can take difficult. It's that you're pathological."

With that, Debbie Turner diagnosed my illness the way a twentieth-century clinical therapist would. One frontal assault espoused. One after another. Each candid gripe cutting me to the core. And she was correct about everything that she said. There wasn't a foul tip that I disagreed with. What could I say? I kicked in our Zenith television set when I lost a Wichita State basketball game in the final seconds. I cursed out Debbie's best friend, Randy Rich, when she entered my man cave while I was holding my breath, clutching my silver dollar, waiting for a final score. I stopped making love to Debbie when I lost a big game. Sometimes for a whole week. Sometimes for a whole lot longer. I felt dead inside. There was nothing to make love with. And there wasn't a reason to hold Debbie's hand either when my heart was ice.

Things didn't get better.

"Maxine, tell Solomon I have to talk to him. It's important."

"How you doin', Davey boy?"

"Solomon, Debbie and me are havin' a terrible time! She's threatening to move out. You gotta talk to her!"

"I'll schedule her in for Thursday for lunch . . . Oh, before you go, Davey boy, how we doin' on the games?"

I called Solomon again on Tuesday.

"I told you. Thursday I'll have lunch with Debbie. Don't worry. Oh, Davey boy, you got anything special for tonight?"

I called again on Wednesday.

"Are you nuts, Davey boy? Stop worrying."

On Thursday Solomon called me. "Davey boy, I forgot all about it! Today I'm having lunch with President Jimmy Carter. I can't see your girlfriend. I can't see her tonight either. I'm having a problem with my factory in Puerto Rico. I must get there tonight. Oh, before I go. Got anything special coming up?"

Three days later, I heard from Solomon.

"I just returned from Puerto Rico, Davey boy. What's doin'?"

"Debbie's moved into the Franconia Hotel."

"That's too bad. How we doin'? Keep pickin' winners, Davey boy. Take it easy."

After Debbie moved into the Franconia Hotel, I stood on the icy street outside of the crummy building every weekend night that winter, waiting to see what time she got home or if not home, to see where she was going, who she was snuggling up with, and when I found out, I acted like the barbarians I worked with. I threatened the fellow's life! I was as bad as that. I'm not going to give myself the benefit of the doubt. I was an animal. I was as sick as any of my mobster friends. "Pathological!" That's what Debbie called me.

Now, I'm in my study, sweeping the floor with memories as I march into my eighties and trying to figure out what to tell Elizabeth about my life. What an impossible task Debbie Turner had with me. Debbie was a wonderful young woman. And I befriended her. Embraced her. I melted as only a son-of-a-bitch who doesn't trust his left hand can trust, and I did Debbie Turner wrong. I have to face it.

Memories keep coming up in the middle of my nights as I toss and turn, adjusting my pillow, thinking of the kind of seducer I was. Never in my entire history of tears and regrets have I felt that I did Debbie Turner anything other than wrong. I must ignore all the cheerful stuff and sentimental crap that I write. I can be as brutal as that pig, Weinstein.

Debbie had a better heart than most, an inner life that glowed with joy, and was engaged to Michael Edison, as decent a young fellow as you would ever want for your son-in-law. And I never stopped seducing her. Never stopped.

In our final parting, Debbie was direct. "I was in love with you, David. You were the older man all girls fall for. I should have protected my marriage to Michael. I should have realized that what I shared with you was a young woman's infatuation. Not that young love isn't wonderful but falling in love with you like I did was foolish. I had something solid with Michael. He was my age. He was responsible. He really loved me. We wanted the same things. I made the biggest mistake a young woman can make. I decided I wanted everything. And that's when I telephoned you."

And now, years later, I still acknowledge her health, my sickness. "You have become Hesse's Steppenwolf," she condemned, "leaping from noble to brutal." I just flinched and stared at Debbie while thinking of how correct she was, as in the forefront of my mind was not the distance between the two, but the closeness.

Debbie Turner was right to move on with her life. She was the best of the best of a certain kind of woman, someone whom I just loved being with. She was my happiness pill, and then, I screwed up, as I did so often.

I made the mistake of emailing her. Here is her reply:

> *David. This is in response to your email. I was fortu-*
> *nate. I found the strength to leave you. I have two won-*
> *derful daughters. A considerate husband. My husband*
> *is extremely entrepreneurial. In fact, this week he's*
> *negotiating to buy an NFL franchise. You said you think*
> *of me a great deal. My advice to you is stop thinking . . .*

I think of another woman I mistreated: my mother. It is now over forty years since she passed. Her death was one of the things I never wrote about, kept out of my mind. My dad was at the hospital, beside her every day, during her last week on earth. Most of the time he was sobbing or praying in her hospital room or in the waiting area when the hospital staff worked on her. Those aides, nurses, and physicians provided extraordinary care, the goodness given by strangers. Not family members, but resolute strangers, people that I depended on, people I never saw again. They're the ones who did the heroic work, were the kindest, the most considerate, the most responsible. I don't even know their names or remember what they looked like or whatever else there is that should be etched in stone. What good was I?

The last day I saw my mom alive, she told me, "David, I've never felt this bad." I lived with my parents two of my mother's last five years, and sixteen times during those years she went to Intensive Care. Each time I thought it was the end, but each time my obese (I called her "Fatty") mom survived, came home, and moved on with her life.

The day she died I had a monster bet on a basketball game. During the game, my father called. "Get over here as quickly as possible, David."

I didn't leave the apartment until I had the final score. I knew I wouldn't get to the hospital in time, and I didn't.

When I arrived, I took one long look at my father, Reverend Kalman Lazar, an orthodox cantor. He was praying; that's what he did his entire life, pray. I have never believed in prayer or wearing the Star of David around my neck. Science is what's in my gut, sophistries have always caused me to shiver. I believe in mathematics over faith. Percentages over magical thinking. A tenet of the Las Vegas oddsmakers is that you should lose fifty percent of the games played with the numbers they attach to the game at hand. I believe that you start out with heads and tails and work 24/7 to find a statistical advantage. Prayers don't change a freakin' thing; pickin' winners does! But too many people need to say prayers, live with the delusion that prayers will make a difference, have delusion drilled into their psyches.

I gave my father one of my derisive nonbeliever looks, walked out of the hospital. Never looked back. But all my dismissal of my father's prayers can't keep my mother's voice out of my head. "I never felt this bad before, David." My suffering mom, who was as loving a mother as any son ever had and who had the bad luck to have me for a son. She deserved better, but that was me, that is me, and today, all these years later, I still hear, "I never felt this bad before. Never!"

It was the last time I heard "Fatty's" voice. What do I have to say? I'm still counting $100 bills? What good is that to Mom? I live with it, but that doesn't absolve me from what I did.

My love of books came from Mom.

"David, don't listen to your father. Read Shakespeare."

Mom took my hand and marched me to the public library before I was five. I immediately fell in love with books. The smell. The jackets. At first it was the children's section. By ten or eleven, I was reading John Tunis, devouring all his baseball novels. I hero-worshipped Tunis' protagonists. Feel-good men who were as warm hearted and American as apple pie. It was also my mom who took me to Carnegie Hall to experience the great Rubenstein and Horowitz and so many other iconic artists. It was always Mom. Of course, the novels I read now might be more challenging than Tunis. William Gaddis' *Agapē Agape* isn't fodder for everyone.

When I was growing up, Mom went out with Dad several times a week.

Not once did she ever leave our apartment without first telling me, "Don't I look gorgeous!" Mom was one of the pear-shaped Jewish women who were high middle class and living on the Upper Westside. They were elitist to an extent and ultra-liberal. My mother had silver foxes, leopard skins, a chinchilla jacket, and a full-length magnificent mink coat. Her closets were full of dead animals. She did look elegant when she was wrapped in these furs. Her clothing was always "cantor" appropriate. Her jewelry tasteful, modest. Mom had a kind face, round and forthcoming. Like mine, her chin was double and, at times, triple. There was never a day people weren't comfortable with my mom. A godsend to the sick, a take-charge woman for good causes, president or close to it of so many organizations, from City of Hope chapters to B'nai B'rith to UJA, my mother had her pudgy hands and soft heart administering TLC 24/7. On the phone from nine in the morning until dusk. Always with good intentions, and when she wasn't doing mitzvahs she was taking care of my father, writing his Man of the Year speeches, helping him pick out the right tie, making sure he ate healthy, advising him on his business affairs, his stock portfolio, and she never stopped worrying about her wayward son. That's how it was while I was growing up. I recall it with a smile. I never received anything but unconditional love from Mom and Dad. As for meals, her cooking was strictly kosher, everything you could want outside of pizza, cola, non-kosher hot dogs, Chinese. We ate strictly by the cantor's rules. Three substantial meals, and when I was in high school, sandwiches that were lunch enough for five.

My father was a grave man, orthodox but not to a fault, with no woman but my mom from the day they met. I think he met her when she was still a student at Barnard, but I could be wrong; it might just as easily have been when she started teaching at the college. Dad was already a superstar in his cantor's world. A great catch. Steadfast, honest to a fault, as moral as Arthur Miller, handsome, stunning, more like a Yiddish movie star, but as decent a guy as one could hope to find. He was a chaplain during WWII. He was a Ten Commandments guy for his entire life and a Joe Louis, Bing Crosby, and Lou Gehrig fan. So why wasn't I more like him?

To this day, I do not have an answer.

But I'm thinking of 1978, when my father was on his last legs and down to sixty-five pounds. The president of his synagogue visited him in his hospital room. In his right hand, he firmly gripped six of my father's LPs, which he wanted Dad to autograph for Israel. The fellow was in good faith. He always revered my dad. The president was round with an artful mustache. He presented himself with kindly authority. Always wore one of those ancient vest-pocket Howard watches and communicated lukewarm decency to his business associates as well as to his constituency. Shrewdness conjoined with a love of God. Pretty hard to do, I think. President Baum managed to make his restrained words sound as if he was juggling all the answers. He stepped closer to my father's hospital bed.

"Kalman," he said, "Your music will live on forever. I have arranged for these albums of yours to be donated to the great libraries in Israel. They will be part of our heritage for the next thousand years."

My dad peered up at President Baum. A flicker of light came to his weary eyes. "Schmuck!" he shouts. "Screw my music! I'm dying!"

Is that how I will go out?

Doubtful.

CHAPTER 10

In the extreme lower right corner of collage number one, I see the photograph of Stanley "Duke" Banks in 1942. Duke entered Pubic School 54 that year. From kindergarten through the sixth grade, he was my constant companion. It now seems strange, but neither Duke's parents nor mine ever discussed Adolph Hitler or the war during those years. Then, both of us went on to P.S. 165. One year later, we were transferred to the brand new, shiny Booker T. Washington Junior High School. From there we went to Lincoln Park High School. Stanley and I were average students. The two of us went on to NYU and four years later, in 1958, graduated without distinction. In those days, it was a nothing accomplishment to get a B.S. degree at NYU. Duke was a great-looking young man. I was fair to middlin'. We always competed for women. Not so with sports. We were both terribly inept in all athletic endeavors. Maybe the very worst on our block. Maybe the entire neighborhood. We were always picked last or next to last. Both of us had our feelings hurt just about all the time. When I was small, I would race home and cry over my athletic inadequacies. Stanley idealized his older brother, Stump, who was working full time at Leventhal's, a neighborhood deli.

"Stump is a great athlete, a Latin scholar, a great boxer . . . a great . . . " Duke would say.

Stanley's dad was a leather goods salesman. His mother a housewife. A chatty affable woman as obese and effusive as my mom. Both women were good friends.

Duke never had any great ambition. I think he realized from the beginning that his life would always be somewhere in the middle. The way he figured it, having a few bucks in his pocket would help him to be cool with the ladies. Duke had Troy Donahue looks, and he posed a great deal. His blue eyes, long neck, deliberate silences, enigmatic posturing, and squinty gaze always seemed to work with women. At NYU frat parties during our freshman year, Duke and I experienced virginal connections with coeds. On our way home on the A train, Duke would invariably exclaim, "Rack it up for experience." We always ended up on our street corner with each other.

Years later, after Leslie, had swept her broom and discarded me, I would mutter to myself in the middle of the night, "I don't need any more experience."

Stanley Banks went on to work for the William Morris Agency and soon represented one super young comic, a dude who, as soon as he hit full stride, left Duke. "I'm sorry, brother, but I feel more comfortable being represented by a Brother."

That dude became a superstar. In fact, he ended up in Hollywood making movies, but right after he did, he blew himself up in his kitchen freebasing meth.

As for Stanley, never again did he find a talent of any significant magnitude. He worked most of his life, voted regularly, never married, didn't have children, lived from the age of twenty-six in the same rent-controlled apartment on the Upper Westside.

Recently I ran into him at the Fairway Market.

"Do you still shop here?" I asked.

"Of course."

"Do you still cook your own meals?"

"Of course."

"Do you ever eat out?"

"Never."

"Do you ever take cabs or call for an Uber?"

"Why should I?"

"Have you ever gone to Paris?"

"Why would I want to go there? The Hudson . . . The Seine—it's all just water."

Duke's thick wavy hair is all gone. His face is bruised by age spots. His skin is violated by tags, furrows, and creases. Duke saved most of his pennies. He was always frugal. "I'm going to leave what I have to my brother's children. That comes to around a hundred and forty large."

It's unreal the way Duke and I went from kindergarten to eighty in such different ways. Rotten though I've been, I'm glad my life wasn't like his.

I'm thinking back to my days learning to handicap. One of the things that kept me going, besides Debbie Turner, was my life as Broadway

Dave, rubbing elbows with movers and shakers, celebrities. January 4, 1973 we were at Solomon's steakhouse. Shecky Greene and Totie Fields had left the table with Solomon's wife. Spacey Shirley MacLaine was talking about living in another century. Stickers was there, too, trying to convince two suits to invest in an outdoor concert he wanted to produce. As usual, the soft-spoken Stickers was telling one bald-faced fib after another. Stickers wasn't unconscionable, but he was without symmetry. What did he have going for him? He was lovable. More so than just about anyone. How could you dislike Stickers? All he wanted was to take his 300 pounds of jelly and parade over to the Stage Deli. "I can give you two fellows thirty percent of the entire production . . . "

Joe DiMaggio sat with us. "What's doin', Joey boy?" Solomon Lepidus bellowed. A second later he said, "Can you imagine that, Joey boy? I'm willin' to put up eight million in real dollars to buy the Yankees and Paley turned me down. That Steinbrenner! The shipping guy from Ohio! CBS is selling the New York Yankees to him!"

"Solomon," I said. "You were turned down because *The Times* exposed how you were laundering money for organized crime figures."

"Them dirty whores! Let them try to prove it!"

Stickers was over ninety when he passed. At one time, he was a giant in the music business. In 1964, Stickers brought The Beatles to Carnegie Hall, and in August 1965, he brought those four English lads back and created history by presenting them at Shea Stadium. Yet Stickers' real story was the second part of his life when he went from fantasy, fame, and triumph to the real.

Stickers was a close friend of Sinatra. Frank had told him, "Nicky DeFrancis is the greatest piano bar singer I've ever heard." Stickers waddled over to Jilly's one night and was soon making it his business to frequent the saloon weekly to hear DeFrancis' extraordinary versions of "Foggy Day in London Town" and "That's Why the Lady is a Tramp." One night at Jilly's, Stickers met a hatcheck girl, Sally Baldwin, a twenty-one-year-old from Eugene, Oregon. For the forty-three-year-old Stickers, it was love at first sight. He was too shy to speak to Sally.

Then Solomon Lepidus took charge. "Stickers, I invited Sally to my steakhouse. You get your fat ass over there. You'll have your shot." Sally and Stickers had several children, whom Stickers adored. It was fun and games for the entire family for a while. Then, Stickers' successes dried up. Debt became a way of life. Stickers was oblivious to the humiliations his wife suffered, his children's struggles, the price the entire family paid for his dreamer's lifestyle.

"I'm going to make it bigger and better, Solomon," he would say each Sunday when we met for bagels and lox. At forty, Sally looked haggard, more beaten down than Stickers. Their children . . . Benjamin, the youngest, hoarded nickels and dimes, stuttered, rolled his eyes, gritted his teeth, kissed his father less and less. Brian, the middle son, raced to his room every time I visited with groceries. The boy would lock his door and refuse to come out until I had left the premises. Stickers' daughter, Melissa Joy, hugged her father all the time. "My dad's the greatest pop in the entire world!" she would tell me. Melissa Joy had anorexia by the time she was fifteen. Stickers was oblivious to the damage he caused. Maybe I was just as guilty. Never once did I ever confront Stickers with any of this. Like all our gang, I went along with Stickers' delusional, "I'm going to make it again, bigger and better, fellas!"

Stickers never raised his voice and never took a drug. His bad faith was always covered up by his obesity. His impenetrable blubber, charm, and presentation were all that he had to offer.

"I've been speaking to Senator Bill Bradley. I told the senator that I'm going to need his help, that I'm on the verge of breaking through one more time and when I do, I'm going to produce an outdoor concert to promote peace and brotherhood worldwide."

Being broke is no way to live. The real always catches up with you. Like Elizabeth asking about Evan Strome, about my life.

Or like when Solomon Lepidus asked me to take him on as a partner in my handicapping. After I moved out of my parents' apartment, I took a four-hundred-square-foot studio. I worked the basketball season that year. I walked away with real money. After that, the phone didn't stop ringing. I was thirty-seven years old.

"I hear you took in a few partners, Davey boy," Solomon said on the phone. "I'm going to give you an opportunity, Davey boy. You'll have access to my sources, my outs, my money! Davey boy, be at my office at 1:00 P.M."

Though I had known Solomon Lepidus since I was twenty-four, this was the first time I had seen this side of him full-blown. I had gotten the gist of the man and put two and two together. I wasn't an idiot, but during all those years, I had never imagined this kind of ugliness. Sickness was there. Deep-rooted malevolent universal hunger and greed. I knew for me to accept him was a conscious leap to the other side.

Catholics call it hell. I call it The American Plague.

I knew I couldn't say no. I didn't want to say no. A large part of me was flattered. When I arrived at Solomon's office, Solomon took his thumb and forefinger and pinched my ear. Hard! (Was it a father thing? My own cantor dad used to pinch my ear, much like Solomon.) Then he pulled out of a desk drawer two six-inch wads of rubber banded C-notes. Telephone numbers would be the kind of bets that I'd now be able to make. I thought of Solomon Lepidus more as my dad than my own father. I thought of him as a "champion amongst men."

"I can't have lunch with you today, Davey boy. But tomorrow night we'll meet at my restaurant."

I didn't want to leave. I was disappointed.

"On second thought, Davey boy, walk with me."

We left his office. The building itself was a converted warehouse with thousands of feet of loft space on every floor. Solomon called it his factory. On the second, third, and fourth floors at least 150 to 200 people hunched over benches. We took a private elevator to the fifth floor, stepped out of the boxcar, and entered a corridor. I followed Solomon on a catwalk at least 300 feet long at the end of which stood an employee in paramilitary khakis and holding a semi-automatic weapon. He waved to Solomon. We climbed a narrow pathway to the top floor. It looked like a vacant parking lot. Solomon opened a door. Then he took a key from his suit pocket and turned a lock in another door. Inside a dimly lit room, a man shook his head. "Mr. Ressler ain't cooperating, Mr. Lepidus," he said with a German accent.

Solomon had introduced me to Jason Ressler at his restaurant. We had had dinner together more than once. Solomon referred to Ressler as "the Schemer." Had pinched his ear just as he had pinched mine. Now, Ressler's jaw was broken. His brow gashed. His arms cuffed. I looked away. Grew nauseous. I peered at Solomon. He appeared to be a beast more than the affable champion amongst men that I had idealized since I was twenty-four.

Ressler was sitting on a straight-backed iron chair in the middle of the enormous room. Around his narrow neck was a Star of David. The

German man had a silver crucifix around his own thick neck. The rest of the room was empty except for a bottle of vodka on the cement floor.

"I wanted you to see this, Davey boy," Solomon said to me in an enthusiastic voice. "Your mom and dad never schooled you in this kind of stuff. But I think now that you're starting to earn a living, it's time you became educated." He grinned.

"I'm proud of you, Davey boy. You could say I'm even impressed." He paused again, and then said in a less enthusiastic tone, "You're just beginning to climb Mount Gamble, and, it's time for you to—" Again, he stopped. "You know what I always say, Davey boy. First you make your living. Then you live your life. You're ready!"

Twenty-six years later, on my third date with Elizabeth Dunn, I told her the story of Jason Ressler. She got up from the sofa she was sitting on with her three cats and raced out of the room. She refused to return. I kept pleading with her to return. I did an about face and said, "I'm just kidding. You know I'm a fiction writer. This is all make-believe."

But that night, Elizabeth didn't allow me to hold her hand or kiss her lips when I said good night. I decided that from then on I would be duplicitous.

"Mendacity is my watchword," I mumbled to myself.

"Prevarication will be my SOP," I said when I cabbed it home.

As I paced my rooftop until dawn, I repeated, "Fuck you, world! I'm free! Fuck you, world! I'm free!"

That's what handicapping and all that went with it has brought me. Freedom. But do I stay the course of duplicity, mendacity, and prevarication? If I go down the honest road, I'll be alone, no Elizabeth, no Liam. That's a freedom I don't want.

I focus my eyes on another snapshot on my wall: a woman, physically faultless. It's my first wife, Leslie, who before me, had everything going for her but for a while I foolishly decided I was a better fit than her Ivy League millionaires or any of her previous CEO husbands. How I remember the details of 1969, the last year of our marriage.

Leslie called me at the Welfare Department. "I'm throwing out your manuscript on American racism. I'm burning that nigger-loving book."

In a panic I ran out of the office, caught the subway at 125th Street and Lexington Avenue, and was down to 59th Street in minutes. I sprinted the four blocks north and two long blocks east to the Regency Towers, our apartment building. At our door, I fumbled with my keys until I finally turned the lock. Leslie was wearing a snug knit skirt, a form-fitting sweater, and, as usual, she was looking like a piece of ass. Between her lips was a Viceroy; in her right hand a half-full glass of Russian vodka. She smirked. I pounced at her, grabbed her hair. She splashed my face with the drink. I raised my hand. I closed my fist. "I burned your manuscript," she hissed.

Half-crazed, I cocked my arm. I couldn't do it.

I headed straight for the toilet bowl and puked.

Many more incidents occurred during our final year as husband and wife.

When Leslie and I separated, both of us were wiped out. She couldn't raise her arms to wash a dish. I couldn't lift a postage stamp.

Of course, it was delicious to walk out on my rooftop terrace at midnight in the late 1970s and shout at the top of my lungs, "FUCK YOU, WORLD, I'M FREE!"

So what lesson do I draw from that? If I were to live my life over again, the only thing I'd change would be to not marry Leslie. But if I hadn't married Leslie, I'd never have had the strength and determination to master handicapping. I wouldn't have the money—and the freedom—that I enjoy now.

What is that life? It's a call from Elizabeth. She read to me the latest teacher reports on our son. The reports are glowing. Liam is a great student, a conscientious, well-meaning citizen on campus. A favorite of all his teachers. The words made me proud. It's my life now. Being proud of my son. Living in the magnificent quiet glow of a slow-moving marriage. I'm content. I was content until Elizabeth asked about Evan Strome.

I often flew to Las Vegas but only to collect or pay. Never once did I have the urge to visit the tables or the available women. On many an occasion, I spent time with Solomon Lepidus at the casinos. Yet I was never enticed. While Solomon might lose as much as a quarter of a million dollars on dice, cards, or on something called Chuck-a-Luck, not once did I put as much as a coin into a slot machine. If I made a wager, I wanted the percentages to be in my favor. I think Liam is going to be even more disciplined when it comes to stuff like that. When he was at the 92nd Street Y pre-school, after he went to the bathroom, he always washed his hands. Even at four years old I never had to tell him to do that. I babble on about my son, as my parents did about me. Everything repeats: bigotry, sadness, mistakes, fear . . . Fear!

I met Elizabeth Dunn ten months after she had come off a recurrence of breast cancer. If I recall correctly, we spoke on the telephone several times. Each one was as crucial as grinding a baseball bat when you come to the plate. You plant your feet. You focus. You concentrate. And then the pitch comes and you either take it or take your swing. I took mine.

Elizabeth was not even close to being talkative, but somewhere in the beginning, I sensed what she had gone through. How terrifying it must have been for her to think about dying. She faced it trembling and alone. I felt guilty that I wasn't there to share her double-mastectomy debate, reconstruction versus going flat. Liz finally decided to go flat.

"I've accepted that my body is mine," she said. "I'm comfortable without reconstruction. The accepting part to me, David, was more important than the surgery I went through. I'm at peace with it. I hope you are, too."

The first year was a gift. Elizabeth One was my all-time favorite. No one in my entire life captured my heart like Elizabeth did. Elizabeth was there by not being there. Elizabeth was there by needing what I had to offer. We started talking and she started voicing opinions with words, intuition, imagination, catastrophic experiences. I heard, listened, and absorbed. I knew Elizabeth One well enough that the gift of life and love flooded me. And I thought during that time that I was on the path to a complete and wonderful friendship, and I was.

To me, Elizabeth is more complete than any woman I've ever known. I am the one who's incomplete. I admit that when I first heard about her reconstructive decision, I thought of Leslie's perfect breasts, Debbie Turner's voluptuous bosom, but then I spanked my brain hard. Grew up. I resolved that what mattered was that I'd found a woman with whom I could connect. The truth is I'm with Elizabeth because it's where I want to be. It's a shared life with parts added and parts missing.

I don't want to lose her.

CHAPTER 11

So many photographs on the wall, at least two dozen of Solomon Lepidus, "everyone's best friend" and mine, too. He was there when I needed him. Not with Debbie Turner, but he was there to save my life. How many times I needed Solomon to intervene. He was street smart, experienced, and unseemly connected. He had the deception of a respectable life: a good wife, children, a place in the community. He knew everyone. He could reach out everywhere to call in a favor. He was Solomon Lepidus. Everyone loved him. He was the disingenuous muscle that I needed to see, talk to, get advice from. He did make Debbie Turner aware that I wasn't just a civil servant, gambler, or the deadbeat I had been during my Leslie years.

"Forget about Debbie Turner, Davey boy. You've got much bigger problems. I just got a call from Willie Alter's office. They say you tried to past post them."

I wasn't a larceny guy, but I wasn't Mister Clean either. What I did was past post one of bookmaker Willie Alter's runners. Gave the clerk a bet ninety-seven seconds after the game had started. I had taken six points on the game, and when I past posted, the score was 13–2 in my favor. Nathan Rubin had gotten away with it. I hadn't. It's a big deal and getting caught at it can send you to the hospital. Or the morgue.

"I'll talk to Willie, but let me tell you, Davey boy, that's not the way to make friends or acquire an honorable reputation. Willie's a good friend of mine. If he wasn't, you'd be getting a beating. And I don't mean anything less than having your skull fractured. You get what I'm saying, Davey boy? Don't do it again! And don't tell me what Nathan Rubin does. What he gets away with is only because, in one way or another, he ends up making everyone rich. Now, get outta my office. I gotta make some calls."

Four days went by before I saw Solomon again. I went to his steakhouse. Solomon peered at me. "I guess you heard what happened. That runner of Willie Alter's who screwed up your bet. He was hit by a car on 10th Avenue and 18th Street at two in morning. Now, Davey boy, what else can I do for you?"

I use the word "handicapping" when I mention my work because it's euphemistic. It doesn't come close to hinting at the carnage my life involved, something Elizabeth never suspected before she read about Evan Strome.

"Solomon, what do you think I should do?"

But I didn't need Solomon Lepidus to sanction my behavior. I wasn't a wimp, who prayed for a solution. I took the matter into my own hands. How many times I aggressively, forcefully, brutally collected. How many times I motivated myself by recalling Leslie Kore's words. "You're a loser, David. A real man would make money." As incredulous as it sounds, I used Leslie as fuel. I did things that others wouldn't do. Couldn't do. Would never do. I could spell them out one by one. I never told even those I loved about many of my deeds.

For instance, one time one of my beards walked out with $2,200 that belonged to me. He pulled what we call in the trade "a claim." He said. "You didn't tell me to bet on Florida State. You told me to bet against Florida State."

I collected my winnings. I carried a brain and a soul that was as unrecognizable to others as it is to me. At times I did terrible things, things I don't regret. I was climbing Mount Gamble. Each step in the climb was a necessity. I sound like a sick man. I am. I was. I shared my decisions with no one. Solomon Lepidus was there, but I owned some of the brute force. He wasn't part of all of it. Many times, I didn't ask his permission or his advice. I acted on my own.

The first time there was a hint of carnage was with a decent family man, Benjamin Futterman, a bookmaker, who had gone bad. Bookmakers can lose as much as compulsive gamblers. Some *are* compulsive gamblers. Benjamin Futterman was. I didn't know that when I started feeding him bets that were larger than he could handle.

I went to his Forest Hills apartment. His wife opened the door. I asked to see Futterman.

"He's not here," she said.

I pushed her aside. Searched the apartment. Every closet. Two bathrooms. The three children's rooms. I found Futterman trembling behind an oak desk in his eleven-year-old daughter's room.

I carried a billy club in those days. It was a gift from a friend of

Solomon's. Champ Holden. I'll talk about him later. It was the first time I ever went over the line. At least, my line. I remember it was a learning tree for me. I cut off a branch and realized that to be successful, I would have to do much more than calculate numbers, analyze reports, get the best odds and line, manage every dollar. It would be war, and in war people are hurt. Benjamin Futterman was a collectible entity. He owed me. He paid me. After that there were others who required me to live a life of sickness, bottom-line greed, so that I could salvage what I had won. Handicapping it was. Handicapping it wasn't. At times I had to do things I haven't revealed to anyone, certainly not to Elizabeth, seldom even to my conscious self. I keep it all inside. A deep, dark, nonverbal secret that only part of me knows. The rest of me is out there with all the civilized people. Acting normal. Being normal. Being the man I want to be. Most of the time I succeed. That was the man Elizabeth knew and loved. The man without the dark secret.

No dark secrets with my son Liam. This morning he texted me that he's been selected to represent Choate in a robotics competition. His robot won him a major trophy last year. Now he's going to be leading the team. I joyously text Squirt back telling him how proud of him I am. I text Elizabeth in North Salem to tell her how I feel more warmth and joy inside for our son's accomplishments than I ever did for mine. After I finish the text, I go to the kitchen and pour myself a glass of chocolate milk. I think of how I got to where I am. I think of Nathan Rubin and his chalk-colored hair, his dwarfish features, his dentures and cackle and peccadilloes. I think of all the ice cubes and walnuts that he shoved up his mistress' butt every Thursday afternoon.

What a different life.

I send Liam another text. "I'm proud of you, son . . . so proud . . . "

I wrote a nonfiction book I titled *Solomon's Pledge* about Solomon Lepidus at sixteen. It was inspired by how in the 1930s, Solomon and Stickers would travel from the Bronx to Germantown on East 86th Street in Manhattan to break up Nazi Bund meetings orchestrated by Indian Joe McWilliams and fueled by "the Radio Priest" Father Coughlin's broadcasts and his National Union for Social Justice pamphlets of hate. Those jingoistic pamphlets ended up in Yorkville bookstores and other Bund locations. It was teenaged Solomon Lepidus who was the most combative in destroying this swill.

Stickers told me, "Solomon might have only been sixteen at the time, but he was our leader, the most determined of all of us. We fought with baseball bats and chains to break up those Bund meetings."

When I wrote *Solomon's Pledge*, I interviewed several of Solomon's boyhood friends, including Sam, a slight, hunch-shouldered old man. (I never was told his last name.) He looked like your neighborhood tailor from the 1950s. He invariably sat in Solomon's office in a far corner reading a newspaper or just minding his own business. The rumor was that Sam was out of federal prison. At Solomon Lepidus' request, he'd killed a prison inmate, a Nazi Bund fiend. Sam, like the other people I interviewed, agreed that Solomon was a born leader.

"All us boys followed Solomon in those days," Stickers told me. "Those who are still around still do!"

I, too, followed that complex man, at least some of the time. Too much?

It's not only men who can be complex, and not only men who fooled me. Fooled me? Was I a fool to expect simplicity? Sure.

I thought Debbie Turner was as unsullied and as much of an apparent winner as Secretariat was in the home stretch in the Belmont. Nothing to worry about with Debbie Turner. "You're my best friend, David," she would say and start blushing. When I touched her inverted nipples, she'd gasp. I loved Debbie Turner and that prick Nathan Rubin knew it. He jumped her one night. Debbie didn't have a chance. What can I say? I didn't give up our partnership. I was making money. Debbie Turner wept for weeks. "I don't understand you . . . I don't understand you . . . " She sobbed night after night.

But that was me. I almost don't understand myself either.

And as crazy as it sounds, Debbie went from being a caseworker in Harlem to living in my penthouse. From wearing ripped jeans to cover her sticks for legs to wearing elegant designer dresses. Then, six years after Debbie moved in with me, she moved out. I tried to get her to come back.

"The plug has been pulled, David. I have nothing left to give to you."

After Debbie moved on with her life, she bumped into someone at Kennedy Airport. The fellow was a member of the One Percent of the One Percent of the One Percent Club. In a New York minute, Debbie Turner became a billionaire. This kind of serendipity only happens in New York. Perhaps it does happen elsewhere, but I only know New York City. We still have poverty, homelessness, women's issues, housing problems, addicts, street gangs, cancer, a less than perfect health care system, corruption, racism, but we have feel-good stories, too. Debbie Turner, who came to New York from Bethesda, Maryland looking like Anne Hathaway in *The Devil Wears Prada*, met the quintessential one percenter. These things do happen in real life. Look at Melania Trump.

Debbie Turner was not wholesome, well-intentioned, or virtuous. Maybe this is my own sour grapes, but in truth, Debbie Turner was as insincere and ambitious as Leslie Kore. Only Debbie had a more backdoor presentation, and real estate guys and Wall Street guys, CEOs, almost all guys, can be duped by a pretty face, perfect melons, an amicable young woman who appears guileless and non-threatening. She could capture a male heart, whether the male's a college student or a billionaire real estate developer. I wasn't shocked that the nearly unsullied Debbie Turner got what she had fantasized about.

When Debbie arrived at the Welfare Department, all she did was fold her arms over her bountiful bosom and smile, and I bought into the whole package. When it comes to women, men are fools, and I'm not close to the top of the list.

I'm not denying that Debbie Turner was my "happiness pill." I loved her with a full, dumb heart. Thought she was a great person. Perhaps she still is, on a given day. But when friends of mine run into Debbie at elite restaurants like Caravaggio or Harry Cipriani or Per Se, she'll always tell them without blinking, "I think of David all the time; I love David. Please tell him to call me."

That's the kind of insincerity that you get from most people. I just didn't think it would be from Debbie Turner.

I take a breath, two breaths. Resentment? Or do I just want to tell myself I wasn't as bad as I think I was. As I was.

Last night. I watched a TV show honoring Al Pacino. I remember Pacino way back in 1968, at the Astor Place Theatre doing Israel Horovitz's *The Indian Wants the Bronx*. Then, I turned to Leslie and whispered, "That actor's going to be the next Brando." Even before 1968, I had often gone to serious theater. Seeing the great Paul Muni in 1955 in *Inherit the Wind* hooked me on drama. I'm thinking about Pacino instead of what to tell Elizabeth for no reason other than at my age, everything's unwieldy. I no longer have the energy to remain focused. How long would it take me to write a book these days?

CHAPTER 12

I'm squinting at a photo of Amy Cho. I must have a dozen photographs of Amy tucked away in my desk drawer, and four dozen of her incorporated into my collage. Comforting memories because the only person I believe I was good for in my entire life besides Elizabeth was Amy Cho.

It was 1983, when I had achieved what most people would call success. I'd written *American Racism*, a book that you can find in university libraries from Howard to Harvard. I'd written four novels that can go on the shelves with the Big Boys. I'd written a best seller. I'd done things that my mother and father would be proud of. I had beaten down the demons, at least some of them. Had recovered from losing Leslie Kore to traditional values and an Atlantic Ocean filled with sharks and seaweed. Had moved on from Debbie Turner, who had married her billionaire, whom I read about frequently in *The Wall Street Journal*, *Forbes*, and *Crain's*.

I met Amy Cho one night when I was having dinner with friends at George Martin's and got in an altercation with Reggie Jackson. Amy and I spoke at George Martin's bar for perhaps five or ten minutes before I returned to my table. I told Amy what I had told Debbie, "Leslie and I were never on the same page. Hell, we weren't even in the same book. When we walked out of City Hall after getting married, Leslie wanted Japanese and I wanted Chinese. We had an argument. She left in one cab. I left in another. We didn't see each other for two weeks. Believe me, Amy, those were our best two weeks."

Once Amy moved in with me it didn't take her long to realize that I would still be struggling for a dollar if it weren't for my need to show Leslie I could make it.

"Gambling worked for me in a big, big way, Amy," I said. "During these past ten years, I burnished my handicapping bona fides, as my friend, The Colonel, liked to say. I exceeded seventy-four percent in winnings four times."

I even started to blab and brag to Amy about how many millions I had accumulated. Somehow, I managed to stop myself from going too far. "I found the money tree, Amy. Or more aptly put, I found 'God!' in handicapping college basketball. 'Blasphemy!' my father would say if he heard me. 'Life is two and two adding up to faith,' my observant cantor-father preached. For me, Amy, handicapping has added up to a providential five."

Amy was in my life from 1983 through 1988. When she lived with me, I'd peek at her every morning while she was sleeping. Gazing at her face was the perfect way to begin my day.

In the beginning, I nursed Amy back to health. She was only twenty-two but already beaten down by life. The first year we were together, I made sure she received professional help for her dyslexia, and I persuaded her to get her GED. The second year, I convinced her to go to Hunter College. I helped her study, I helped with her term papers. I did my best to keep her motivated.

Before the second year ended, she said, "David, I think I can write my own papers. I'd like to try if you don't mind."

The third year, she made the Dean's List and that, along with my walking her to school every day, are some of my best memories. Those five years with Amy Cho were the happiest years of my life. Of course, it helped that I was making important money. And I was working on a novel, which always pleased me. But it wasn't the money or my writing. It was Amy Cho.

Most people in my life think that I rescued Amy Cho. In truth, it was Amy who rescued me. She provided that exhilarating feeling of wanting to be alive. The two of us didn't do anything that was profound or earth shattering; we just liked each other, were considerate of each other. I guess the absolute truth was we were always there for each other during those five years we shared.

The thing that I recall more than anything is the day Amy played her first basketball game for Hunter College. She raced onto the court, got involved in the antics; then, when one of her teammates passed her the ball, she put her head down and started dribbling. The thing was that Amy drove straight to the opposing team's basket.

"David, I don't think I'm very good at basketball," she said to me after the game.

There are always watershed moments in a friendship. There was one in our relationship.

I was at my peak as far as picking winners went. Counting wads of bills almost every Tuesday. I would collect them with my bodyguard, Champ Holden, at my side, from two, three, or as many as a dozen bookmakers and beards who owed me for the week's bets. When I returned home, I would toss the winnings on the bed and tell Amy, "Start counting."

As she did so, I would begin to kiss her brow, her cheeks, her ears, her bare shoulders, her knees, thighs. Everywhere. Invariably she would lose her concentration.

"David, now I have to start all over again!"

Those were the best of times. On one of those Tuesdays, Amy said, "David, you're almost fifty. You've stopped exercising and when you fall asleep at night, your breathing sounds kinda funny." She paused. "I think it would be a good idea if you got a complete check-up."

The doctor looked exactly like Peter Lorre in *Casablanca*. Only this wasn't Ugarte; it was Dr. Paul Schweitzer, a concierge cardiologist, whom Amy had found for me. I forked over a large check for Dr. Schweitzer to take me on as a patient.

I spent an unpleasant two-and-a-half hours with Dr. Schweitzer. He conducted the most comprehensive examination I had ever experienced. Even did an echo-something-or-other on me. When Dr. S. finished, he asked, "Do you want your wife with you in my office when I tell you what I think?

"We have no secrets," I said.

"You have six months to a year."

I bit my lip. Reached for the 1877 silver dollar that I carried with me at all times. To this day, I have callouses on my palm from clenching that coin. I gripped it tightly every time I got a score. I tried like hell to control my emotions. Amy was already sobbing.

"I don't think you have any kidney problems. Your lungs seem fine. It's your heart. Your heart seems to me more like that of a man of seventy-five with heart disease." Dr. Schweitzer stopped. Stroked his chin. "It's heart disease all right." He said I must have a sleep study done. "I'm sure you're going to have to wear a mask."

Amy reacted immediately. "David's been wheezing through the night, Dr. Schweitzer. Sometimes it seems as if he stops breathing."

Dr. Schweitzer nodded his head. "Your husband needs to have an

X-ray. Also, some blood tests. And make sure he takes these medications I'm prescribing." On and on he went.

In all that time, neither one of us thought it necessary to contradict Dr. Schweitzer about our marital status.

I glanced at Amy. What do you say to a barely twenty-five-year-old woman who's in love with a man twice her age? What do you tell yourself? I tried to take a few deep breaths. Process the electric waves of my own mortality. My first instinct was predictable: I didn't want to die. I loved life. I loved Amy. My life was great. I couldn't ask for anything more. Now this!

My second response was less weepy. Solomon Lepidus would warn me just about every other week, "Be prepared, Davey boy. Guys who live by the sword usually die by the sword."

I certainly was handicapping by the sword. Cutting corners. Outwitting mobsters. Collecting in brutal ways when necessary. Dying with every loss. It wasn't pretty. I wasn't pretty. I had been expanding my dehumanizing business for fifteen years. The more that I expanded my business the more I had to look over my shoulder. Check under restaurant tables for wires, sit with one eye always watching the crowd. When it came to writing checks, I had to be extremely careful. By that time, Nathan Rubin was one of my two largest partners. He sent over one of his Metropolitan Cable Company technicians to sweep my "special phones" every week. These "special phones" were located on my rooftop during the college basketball season. I used them from 11:00 A.M. until one the next morning, seven days a week.

Winters in New York City, with the wind chill, are painful. During the seventeen-week college basketball season, I would be on my rooftop receiving calls from beards with information on injuries, changing lines, confirmation on bets, and much more. The calls were synchronized, precise, coded. If a beard made even one mistake, he was gone. During my prime years, I'd begin in early November with over 100 beards. By December 15th, I would have fired half of them and replaced them with a fresh crop. Mistakes were not, could not, ever be tolerated. It meant dollars. Important dollars. I was cold. Had to be. Needed to be. I masterminded all of it. Placed these beards across the country. Mostly on college campuses, because that was where the information was. Who's having problems with his girlfriend? Who missed practice because of a scratch or a turned ankle? Who . . . And what about the coaches? Beards relocated from Bowling Green, Kentucky to Kalamazoo, Michigan to Gary, Indiana to Manhattan, Kansas to Boston, Massachusetts to Athens, Georgia. On paradisiacal campuses. With students like my son, Liam, innocently cheering for their schools. I used bookmakers from Las Vegas to New York to Toronto, Canada to Costa Rica.

Fuck the schools! Fuck the students! Fuck the players! As far as I was concerned, every player who had ever lived could drop dead if I lost the game. Everyone was the enemy. It was war, a war in which I was taking no prisoners, a war in which I wouldn't be a prisoner.

I had expanded! And with expansion came contracts on my head. By this time, Solomon Lepidus had had to step in two more times to save my ass. And there would be several more life-and-death "contracts" on me in the coming years. But in 1987 there were only five. And even the well-connected Solomon Lepidus had difficulty neutralizing them. Bookmakers didn't like people like me. Not as a person but me as an opponent. I have no hard feelings. People are people. Greed! Ego! Animals! Money! In those things, most of us wear the same scarred skin, are in the same war. I looked over my shoulder every day.

Stress became my middle name. Amy started calling me "Mister Stress." I tried to be careful. More and more, I was using code names, secret agents improvising techniques and mechanisms to thwart a constantly evolving and murderous enemy. My strategies made it almost impossible for my enemies to know how much I was getting down. I might be wagering $50,000 on a basketball game when divided by, let's say, twenty-five bookmaking offices and telephoned in by, let's say, twenty-five of my beards, it seemed as if I were wagering no more than $2,000 on any of them. At one time, I had forty-nine bookmakers. One hundred and twelve beards. And, of course, I had my own wits and Nathan Rubin and Solomon Lepidus as resources as well.

I can honestly tell you that "I lived by the sword, but I didn't die by the sword."

Dr. Schweitzer continued, "You must lose fifty pounds. Stop eating! Eliminate stress! You must do this and that, and we'll know a whole lot more after you've had those tests I'm ordering."

Dr. Schweitzer walked over to his desk. Looked at some notes he had scribbled during that two-and-a-half-hour siege.

"I don't think any of the results are going to be good," he said.

I clenched my silver dollar. Took a quick glance at Amy. She looked as if she were five years old.

When we returned home, I told Amy that I was going to make long-term provisions for her. That she wouldn't ever have to worry about money.

"David, you should quit gambling right now. I don't care about money. I care about you."

I started to pontificate B.S. I espoused something I had read by a Holocaust survivor on how Americans are never prepared for death. For Americans, he said, death comes as a shock. They're cowards, he said. I continued babbling through the night. What brought me to a halt was when Amy stood up tall on top of our bed.

"You're not going to die, David. You're going to get better. You're going to eat better, exercise, and start living less like a crazy man."

I yanked Amy down on the bed. We made love.

I loved Amy Cho.

Every one of those days was lyrical, and they stayed precious until eleven months later when she said, "I have something to tell you."

"David, the last thing I would ever want to do is cause you pain. When I think of your pain, I shudder."

Amy Cho moved out. I couldn't let go.

"I can't handle the pressure you place on me. Christian is a happy person. He's so much easier to be with. We comb each other's hair with our fingers. We go to concerts together, we like the same kind of music, we go clubbing together. You never went clubbing with me, David."

I couldn't let go.

"I know you love me. That's not the problem. At night, I lock myself in the bathroom and agonize over what is missing. Some nights, I masturbate while you are watching a game or writing. Why is it that you aren't aware that something is very wrong?"

I couldn't let go.

"You have to move on. Be strong. You're strong in so many ways. If it wasn't for you, I would never have survived. Now you have to be strong for yourself."

I couldn't. A telephone call. A letter. A not-so-chance meeting.

"I upset Christian as much as I upset you. He's also a very good person. He loves me, too. But I've become numb with him, too. I can't go on hurting people, David. I have to stop. I'm scared, and I feel nothing. My body and the rest of me are far apart."

One month later.

"What I want, David, is to not need Christian or you. I want to feel strong and independent. Not be dependent on any man. I have to take time to get to know who I am. I'm so in touch with what you and Christian want that I lose what I want. Why is it, David, that the less I want of men and the more I try to distance myself from them, the more men seem to need me? The closer they try to get?"

Several months passed.

"I'm searching for what the answer is. Not to just run away from you but to move closer because I feel a desperate need to stay away from you and, uhm, that's all I can say right now. That's what I'm feeling. I can't look the other way. I've done that too much of my life—looked away from what I'm really feeling. David, take care of yourself, okay?"

Two months later, Amy returned.

"I thought about what our life would be like if we were married. I'd run my jewelry business, and that would be a full-time job. And you would work on your book. We'd go to the movies together, and the theater, when we had the time. We'd take long walks and talk. You'd read your creations to me and recommend books for me to read, and then we'd talk about them, as well as everything else. We'd travel, too. And, of course, we'd have lots of dinners with Mr. Lepidus and your friends. It would be a nice life. I think we could be happy." Amy's brow furrowed. "I've made up my mind. Let's go down to City Hall today and get married. I'm ready now. Let's jump right in! No, make it the day after tomorrow. That'll give us time to get the blood tests."

We decided to go to the Palm Court in the Plaza Hotel for tiramisu and talk.

"You're my best friend, David, but it's hard for me to remember the rest. I don't know what it is," Amy said anxiously. "I'm not in touch with those feelings any longer." Amy looked up at me. "But we'll get them back, won't we?"

As soon as we returned to the apartment, we sat down on the leather sofa. Amy crossed her arms over her chest. "I know how much I love you. I'll be a good wife. I'll always respect you, do anything you want me to. But do you think I'll ever feel as I did? In those ways, I want to be with you, too."

I gazed at Amy, knowing that I had lost her. I started to say something but then stopped, feeling depleted, knowing what I had set out to say was the only inevitable answer.

"Amy, in a few days, we're supposed to be going to City Hall."

"I know that. I'm ready. This time I won't run away."

I sat there, silently gazing at Amy's face. Finally, I said, "You know, Amy, I no longer have those romantic notions about us; I'm not holding onto them any longer."

Amy's face brightened. "I knew you would outgrow them. You're an intelligent man. You're brilliant! I've learned so much from you. So much of what I am, I owe to you. I knew you would let go of them sometime."

I choked. For a moment, I couldn't speak. Finally, I said, "You're very special to me, Amy. I want you to be happy." Then, I fumbled again as I searched for the right words. When I recovered, I said, "I want you to get the most you can out of life. You know that." Amy stared at me. Perplexed. I felt like grabbing her. Never letting go. I gulped down hard. We gazed at each other.

"David, I love you."

"I know you do," I said, beginning to cry.

Amy lifted herself from the sofa, kneeled in front of me. "David," she said, looking up at me. "If it were ten years, even fifteen, I'd stay with you. I can sacrifice ten or fifteen years. But you're not that old. You're going to live another forty years. I can't sacrifice forty years, can I?"

Amy calmly walked to the closet and took out her night bag. Her jacket. She moved quickly through the foyer. I struggled to find something to say but couldn't.

"David," Amy said. She wiped a tear from her eye and then straightened her shoulders and took several more hesitant steps toward the door. She turned. "I don't know. Maybe it's because I don't think I've finished my relationship with Christian. I mean, you just appeared, and I felt compelled to come back to you. You have a magical hold over me. Maybe if I resolved my feelings for Christian."

"You will, Amy. And I'll wear a tux at the wedding."

"You'll always be in my heart, David—always."

"And you in mine."

I tried to gather myself together one more time. I took hold of her shoulders. "I love you, Amy."

"David, I wanted to give you what you want. I still do, but I just can't." Amy paused, and then her whole face seemed to light up. "When I have a baby, I'm going to give it so much love. The kind I felt I missed out on until you came along. I'll teach it all about spirituality and feeling thankful. I just know it will be a special child. I can feel it even now." She paused again. "I feel great thankfulness that because of your love, I'm now capable of giving life to another person. It's something I'll never forget." I wiped a tear from Amy's cheek. "When I have a child, my child will know you as soon as he's ready to. That I promise you, David Lazar."

I opened the front door and stepped out into the hallway. I took Amy's hand, half pulled her through the door. She began to softly sob.

"Amy," I whispered, "you know I can't take it when you cry."

(My father wiped the feces from my mother's backside when she was dying. He wept salty tears as he cried out, "My life is over without your mother!" My father passed away soon after. I understood my father. I wasn't my father although I, too, cried salty tears.)

"Make a muscle, Amy."

She looked up.

"C'mon! Lemme feel your muscle!"

Slowly, Amy made a muscle.

"Now, let me feel the other arm." She did. "Just as I thought—your wings are strong now. So, fly, Amy Cho, fly!"

A gentle half smile crossed her face.

"My David," she said, "My David." She extended her hand and touched my face. "Goodbye, David," she said. "You're the best." She stepped inside the elevator and flew out of my life, on her own, forever.

CHAPTER 13

A while ago, I went to Bergdorf Goodman to buy a Loro Piana winter coat. On the main floor I saw this young woman behind the counter. She had shoulder-length chestnut hair and a face that belonged to an eighteen-year-old Leslie Kore.

When I told Elizabeth about it, she said, "I know how much it must have killed you, David, to see that woman who reminded you of a young Leslie. It had to eat your heart out. If I could do something, I would. All I can tell you is . . . here I am! Let's go upstairs and have some fun."

I'm well aware of beauty's transcendence. No debate. But I've matured to where surface looks mean very little. As I always tell Liam, "What means something is the beauty that comes from you know where."

Thankfully, I am now able to see the caring and the giving and the kindnesses in a whole person. How could I have been blind for so long to what truly matters? How could we all be so enamored with nonsense? We look at magazine ads! We look at TV commercials! We go to the movies! We look. None of us stop looking.

I'm already telling my son ad nauseam, "Stop looking!"

Last year flew by. It's as if I were on a Metro North train with the stations just whizzing by. The trees I'm passing, the cows I'm spotting, the horses I'm seeing, all of it is a blur. The people I'm thinking about are also a blur. I'm doing the best I can to keep up with the dizzying pace.

When Liam was returning to Choate, I gave him a hug and reminded him, "Keep texting. I'm going to miss you."

I spent some quiet time with Elizabeth. I told her I was happy with Amy Cho.

"Of course, you were happy with Amy Cho. You were making tons of money during those years. You were relatively young. Being a novelist still meant something back then." The two of us just held hands and breathed in the crisp North Salem air.

I called Leslie Kore not long ago.

"I'm glad you called," she said. "I wanted to speak to you in person. I'm nothing like I was all those years ago. You don't know me, David. I now believe in one thing only: no game playing. Yes, you were special. I'm not going to deny that. You had the potential to be a great success in business. The problem was that you never had the courage to try. You're probably still working with filth and sleaze. I did see you. Twice. Once at the American Ballet Theatre. You and Ron Nevins were sitting in the same row as Jackie Kennedy. I was three rows behind you. A second time was at the theatre. I think the musical was *Big River*. I don't remember the year. The Asian woman you were with was almost a child. You looked like her grandfather. So many things about you were off-putting, David. Do you have any other questions? I'm getting quite tired."

"One more, Leslie. Where did we go wrong?"

"I won't continue *that* conversation unless we can establish a genuine rapport. Right now, I'm feeling anxious. My nerves are bad. I'm losing my hair. At night, I have heart palpitations. I take antidepressants. When I feel this way, I go into myself. I disappear. I felt this way every minute of our marriage. Is it any wonder I disappeared? The truth is, David, during our entire marriage, I was always seeking a way out. I gave to you only what I could afford to give. What we shared was pornography. Do you think I possibly could've forgotten how you tried to strangle me? How you lifted me off the ground? Wouldn't let go? If Ron Nevins hadn't intervened, why, you would've . . . "

"Do you remember the cellar?" I asked her.

"Let's go down to my parents' cellar," Leslie whispered, recreating the moment.

I remember her removing her shoes. We tiptoed together down the stairs. The cellar meant privacy.

"Of course, I remember that day, David. We walked on the beach. You quoted Nietzsche aphorisms to me; I recited Shakespeare sonnets. What I recall more than anything else is the blizzard of 1961. I couldn't go home. Everything was shut down. I had to stay at your 56th Street apartment that night. You had Nina Simone playing in the background. We were together in bed, and I started complaining about not having any cigarettes. You jumped out of bed and ran all over the neighborhood looking for a pack of Camels. When you got back, you told me that the snowdrifts were as high as your shoulders. Here's something else I recall: the following morning when I was about to return to my parents' house, you asked me if you could keep my silk blouse under your pillow so that my aroma would be near you. I slipped on your flannel shirt. Wait! I think I still have it somewhere."

Are today's young people's friendships that different than the way Leslie and I conducted ourselves during those seventeen years? Today versus yesterday. No right or wrong. Just is.

I go to see a movie, and then I hobble home. It's a lovely day. Too lovely to take one of those expensive yellow taxis. How average people can afford cabs is beyond me. And yet, in Manhattan, people do. Meters clicking all the time. I'm one of the fortunates who can yell out, "Taxi!" without worrying about the cost. And then I think what I had to do to make my money. Sold my soul so that I could spare myself walking home?

As I reach Columbus Circle, two six-foot-tall identical twins interrupt my thoughts. Now what flashes in my head is 1961. These twins are as perfect as Gunilla Knutsson, Miss Sweden, was when I took her to Jilly's. Nicky De Francis was at the piano bar singing "Foggy Day." Tony Powers was on drums. In 1966, Gunilla was on everyone's TV as the "Take it off—Take it all off!" Noxzema girl.

As pubescent as I was at twenty-four, I walk up to the identical twins and am ready to say, "You two should see how spectacular the city looks from up high. I live in the penthouse down the block."

Though I'm aware of the obscenity of my age, it still seems natural to make a move on these young women. I don't feel like a dirty old man. As I'm about to say something dumb, I see the second twin's look, and out of the corner of my eye, I see how pedestrians walking by are noticing me. I realize how weird it must seem to everyone but me. Elizabeth has warned me a thousand times, "Act your age!"

I shrug. The women keep walking.

It's more than just a geezer's lech. Yes, I'm an octogenarian, yet my awareness—call it a preoccupation—with youth and beauty is still a healthy yearning. The more beauty is missing from my life, the more I long for it. It's not sex, lust, passion, or a love of the chase that's missing. It's beauty. When I'm with Elizabeth, we'll hold hands. Sleep side-by-side. But in the morning, she'll peer at me and gravely ask, "How do you feel?" She worries about me constantly. That's the real violation in being wed to someone who is thirty years younger than you are. I watch as the identical twins walk into the crowd to find their own adventures, and, as they disappear, the loss of their beauty makes me sad, sadder than even when summer disappears.

I keep thinking how the loss of Leslie Kore drove me to handicapping. I made my money through hard work, handicapping the games as if I had three Ph.Ds. from MIT. And once I took off, I had a crew of beards working for me. All these math geniuses scratched their heads at my—for lack of a better word—meta methods. My success wasn't luck. It came from fourteen-hour days, preparation, studying numbers, trends, understanding the game, match-ups, discipline, money management, maximizing and minimizing, going to war, and ultimately picking winners.

Leslie Kore dumped me for the right reasons. I didn't make a living. A caseworker for the city. "What kind of job is that?" Leslie would scream. I wanted to be a novelist. Write the Great American Novel. Leslie couldn't take having an in debt, gambling wannabe for a husband. It doesn't take me much effort to make Leslie sound all bad. Just as I can make myself sound all bad. There is conflict, rage, violence, ambivalence, love in all of us. I didn't put out the trash or bring home the cereal. I stayed out way past two in the morning with friends. Not women! That is one thing I can say. With all the women I've ever loved, including Leslie Kore, I never cheated on any of them. Not once! If I tell you, "I love you," it sticks. I'm lucky that way. The woman I'm with is the woman I want to be with. For almost fifty years, my parents were married. Their lessons in fidelity and devotion and their unconditional love still holds much as a whole truth inside of my psyche.

"What are you screaming for, Leslie? You should be happy for me. If I'm happy hanging out with friends at two in the morning."

Why should a young person such as I was stay home when this city offers unending adventures? So many things to do. So much culture. So much to take advantage of from theater to the Philharmonic to ballgames to friends. Yes, women! So many women! Nines and tens. Even more so today with all the gyms and diets and cosmetics and water bottles and jogging lanes and bicycle paths. Every five or even a three can turn herself into a seven, an eight, or even a nine. As many near-to-perfect specimens being created as if they were on a Henry Ford assembly line. But Leslie Kore was from no one's assembly line. She was a natural ten. So why am I so fucked up? Perhaps because my day has passed me by.

I'm driven to write this to my son.

> To Liam, who is experiencing female issues for the very first time.
>
> I remember, Liam, when I was twenty and my 'first girlfriend,' Sheila, was about seventeen. We had been seeing each other for two-plus years every Saturday night. Every weekend I was taking the BMT subway into Brooklyn to Sheepshead Bay, and then subwaying back to the city with Sheila to see a movie and, if I could afford it, a Chinese dinner, and then back to Brooklyn to take Sheila home, and then about one in the morning, taking my return trip to Manhattan to my own bedroom.
>
> One night after those two-plus years, Sheila told me, "David, I've been thinking a whole lot about us. You're always serious and thinking and reading books and, well, people like that are just never happy. And I want to be happy, David."
>
> And after that jolt, Liam, came a quick goodbye. I didn't see Sheila again until we bumped into each other at Saks Fifth Avenue when she was shopping for her daughter's wedding.
>
> Back to the breakup. I went home and knocked my head against my bedroom wall for two days. For the next three months, I cried myself to sleep every night. Then I met another young woman and things got a whole lot better.
>
> The point is, Liam, even a jaded guy like me started out in 'Rookie Camp.' Was overwhelmed by a female and a depth of feeling. Of course, with your mother,

things are different. Mommy is so perfect that all I can
complain about is her nagging about my staying on my
diet and my exercise lapses. And, of course, with my
relentless aging, there is more of her nagging than ever.

Hobbling over to The Smith this morning. At this stage of my life, it's a supreme effort to walk four blocks. The Smith is my favorite hangout place for coffee and a "scooped" bagel. On the way, I spot a long-legged woman walking in front of me. I can't catch a glimpse of her from the front, but from the back she reminds me of Leslie Kore. So, what do I do? I rush after this woman like a crazy person. I want to see what she looks like.

For the life of me, I can't break into a fast-enough shuffle to catch up to this long-legged woman. She makes every light, and after three blocks I run out of both wind and curiosity.

I phone Liam from The Smith. "No reason for you to be nervous." Squirt is worried about his acne. What's brought this vanity on is that he has a blind date this weekend. I don't know what to say. Just about every time I speak to my teenage son, I feel as if whatever I say is dumb. I get tongue-tied. I started rambling on and on. I mention to Liam everything that pops into my head, and then I think of Leslie Kore.

"The first time I telephoned my first wife for a date, Liam, I left my parents' apartment, walked to a phone booth on the corner. I went to a phone booth because I didn't want my mom or dad to hear me when I spoke to her. I was that uptight, Squirt. I made notes on what I was going to say. Squirt, right now, if I close my eyes, I can still feel myself shaking when I dialed Leslie's number."

"Geeze, Ba, that's exactly what happened to me."

I wonder if I'll ever be able to tell my good and decent son about the day that my bodyguard Champ Holden and I were in a shootout in Harlem.

I am wide awake by 5:00 A.M., having tossed and turned throughout the night. Every second thinking of one thing. How I would approach, which something in my mind believed necessary, this horrible incident with my bodyguard, Champ Holden. A bad choice to start the day with, yet I must start somewhere. I knew I wanted to do this. I had consistently obsessed about doing this. Was I going to reveal this to Liam? To Elizabeth? At the very least, I had to face it myself. This shoot-out in Harlem might be of negligible consequence to everyone else, but to me, it's as paramount as a death in the family.

Champ Holden's pants cuff come to mind. The blood on the bottom of the right cuff, which measured two inches. Champ Holden always wore two-inch cuffed slacks, and, on that eventful day, he did the same. His blood, the color of which was not as red as you would assume but more the color of pavement, was smeared over his cuff like a large blot. It also covered the thigh part of his trousers. A gaping rent in the trousers.

That day I had gone to Angelo Ferrari's office on 117th Street and Pleasant Avenue to collect. Ferrari was one of my heavyweight bookmakers who had the balls to take large amounts on a game without changing the line.

Angelo Ferrari paid me. I stuffed the rubber-banded Franklins into my socks and shook his hand. I didn't count the cash. Never did. Respect is given in many ways. My not counting the money was one of them. Ferrari shook my hand again when Champ and I were leaving. Two of his men grinned, then looked the other way. Champ Holden didn't say a word. He never did. So that wasn't unusual.

Champ walked beside me like he was a Rottweiler. We started west to Park Avenue. As we reached the cutout under the Metro-North tracks, Champ spotted two men walking toward us. Champ immediately reached for his Glock and pushed me flush against the tunnel's brick wall.

Our two adversaries had on unflattering jeans and wore dark gray sweatshirts. They weren't V-necks or turtlenecks or the kind of Polo sweaters that cost me a fortune when I went to Ralph Lauren.

These Mafioso didn't wait to start shooting. Their first round hit Champ in the leg. He kept firing. The Mafioso also had Glocks. I took out my more primitive Smith & Wesson revolver and joined the fray.

Gunshots as noisy as a motorcycle's rumbling filled the territory. Only this wasn't a motorcycle driver's powerful engine—it was two animals on one side and two animals on the other trying to destroy each other. I thought of the bullets and the mud and the blood and the cause of this conflict: the wads of rubber-banded Franklins stuffed in my socks.

These two animals wore mackinaws over their sweatshirts because the weather was awful. Their boots were scuffed and black. One of them had stringy yellow laces on his unpolished boots. I put down the bearded animal who wore the yellow laces. He staggered before he fell. The other guy lay bleeding on the ground.

A minute later I was grabbing for Champ's wrist.

He, too, had been badly wounded. His thigh was oozing blood; so were his neck and arm. It was me who was dragging him, foot-by-foot down the Harlem stones from the middle of 117th Street and Park Avenue to the safer and more protected cover inside the Metro-North railroad tracks.

The entire encounter from its beginning to its very end took no more than three minutes. I clearly remember the dragging part. I'm eighty, and I still remember that day. It happened too many years ago for me to be answerable or take responsibility for it, but it happened, it counts. It's one day in a million in one's life's experiences, but this one was more real, more remembered than most others that I have lived through.

I wasn't sure if the two men were dead or alive. And I never found out if it was a set up by Angelo Ferrari or something these two did on their own.

"It had to be Ferrari, Davey boy," Solomon told me. "He's pissed that you've been collecting all season. What the hell, Davey boy. You don't have to know the rest of it. It doesn't help to know too much."

I want to think more about it, but I can't. For some reason, my mind, like my quill pen, is blotting, it's blurring my memory, the stain is obvious—it won't come out. It never disappears.

I have to confess, at least to myself if not to Liam, not to Elizabeth, that a chunk of me doesn't think it a despicable thing that I was in barbarous shootouts with the men I opposed. Maybe a large chunk doesn't consider my behavior despicable. I was no better than they were. I was probably a whole lot worse considering the advantages with which I had started out. But how many of us went off to war without blinking or thinking? Killed better men than we were?

Leaving those two men on the Harlem pavement is not the only thing I've kept from Elizabeth and Liam. So many times Solomon said, "Let me take care of this problem, Davey boy." And I let him. There were countless problems that Solomon Lepidus took care of for me.

"I've got to get to the Waldorf tonight, Davey boy. I'm giving a speech to raise money for AIDS research." And two seconds later, Solomon was reaching for one of his "special phones" and deciding on someone's life. I was there. I was part of it. I was as responsible as he was. I had choices, too.

"Good" or "dollars"?

There were times I chose "good." There were times I chose "dollars." There were many times I told Solomon Lepidus, "I have to think about it," when he asked me my opinion on how to resolve a problem.

Did I think about it? Not always. Sometimes it was just a way to avoid a decision and let Solomon take care of it for me without my telling him to.

CHAPTER 14

O ne of the reasons there was so much stress in my handicapping life, maybe the main reason, was one that I never told anyone. Not even Amy Cho, and Amy was with me during five of those Hell years, I didn't even mention it to that Peter Lorre double, the cardiologist doc who gave me a final notice if I didn't start to follow his instructions. Much of my stress was caused by Evan Strome.

I met Evan Strome at the Currency Club on 79th Street between Madison and Fifth. It was a private club for card-playing Caucasians and lesser numbers of males of other denominations. It was mainly for men with expensive hardware on their wrists and fingers and Franklins in their pockets, businessmen with hard-bellied and soft-edged skills with which to earn good livings. Nathan Rubin and The Colonel, Morty Lefko, were members. Three things about The Colonel: he had a huge belly, a Havana cigar, and a voice as warm and friendly as your childhood memories of your Uncle Tommy. Nathan Rubin was not. Besides them, I knew other club members: Oscar Strome, Isaac Pizer, Judge Elmer Russo, "Big" Ed Litt, who was five foot one and the club's current president, "Little" John Flynn, who was six foot six and a retired commissioner of something or other, and on and on.

Evan's father, Oscar, was the superstar at the Currency Club. He was a card-playing shark almost on par with Nathan Rubin. Nathan Rubin rarely had dinner at the club and never, to my knowledge, played cards there. Ditto Solomon Lepidus. The Colonel did. Many nights I had dinner at the Currency Club with The Colonel and his wife, Sylvia. As for Oscar Strome, he was a bookmaker who had three clients with whom I was familiar: Lepidus, The Colonel, and Rubin. I, too, had called in bets to Oscar Strome, not at his home in Scarsdale or at his office on Jane Street, but only at the club.

Oscar was always there, from two in the afternoon through din-nertime. When he wasn't playing cards, he was fielding bets. As for

Strome's card playing, it was not a hobby; it was his vocation. What he didn't earn as a bookmaker, he earned as a card player.

On the occasion I first met Evan Strome, I was at the club to collect some money that Oscar Strome owed me. While I was there, an incident that seemed of little consequence at the time took place.

"Hi, Oscar. I can only stay for a minute," I said. "You have a package for me?"

"I do, kid," Strome answered unpleasantly.

From his jacket pocket, he took a bulging envelope.

As Strome handed me the envelope, The Colonel took his Havana out of his mouth and said, "I can't find my cigarette lighter. My wife is going to murder me. She just got it for me. It's from Harry Winston's. Has my initials on it and everything!"

The Colonel bent down with great effort. Looked under the table. It wasn't there. He started moving drinks, ashtrays, chips, and cash around on the card table. Still, nowhere was his lighter to be found.

"I'm dead meat when I get home," The Colonel muttered.

Evan Strome, Oscar's son, was at the table. I engaged Evan in conversation as The Colonel continued making a fuss over his missing cigarette lighter.

"I hear you're going to Michigan State in the fall. Congratulations. I always wanted to go to a Big Ten school."

Evan Strome, a rail-thin drink of not-so-clean water with pointy teeth, grinned at me. He said he was looking forward to going to school in East Lansing and that Nathan Rubin had a great deal to do with paying his tuition. "I worked like a slave to achieve the necessary grades and like a serf for Nathan Rubin," he said.

"What are you going to major in?" I asked.

"I'm thinking of going into sports management. I want to represent basketball players who turn pro. There's a whole lot of money in baskets, with TV and marketing coming into their own. I think player salaries will be sky-rocketing by the time I graduate."

"Do you know any players right now?" I asked.

"Yes, I do." Evan spat out the names of four very solid New York City basketball players, players certainly good enough to have marginal careers either in the NBA or in Europe.

"How come you know these guys?"

"I played high school ball at Stuyvesant. I also played in the Rucker tournament in Harlem for the past two years, and I was on an AAU team last summer. I also know several coaches. I think that gives me a head's up to get somewhere in the business."

The Colonel sneezed.

"Gesundheit! God bless you," I uttered.

Ash from The Colonel's cigar dropped on the card table. He took his stubby hand and wiped it off.

"Let's stay in touch, Evan. Take care, and please do return Mr. Lefko's lighter to him."

I left shortly after that.

Evan Strome became one of my beards. He was great at the job. If I was a good handicapper, Evan Strome was just as good at bearding. We were on the same team. I counted on him for information. I relied on him for getting me down with bookmakers at the best numbers. I depended on him. My business grew because of Evan Strome. My bankroll multiplied. The bottom line is that because of Evan Strome, I made money. But . . .

I heard a New York cardinal talking today, the chubby one who wears a white robe with the red-and-gold trim and who has all the answers. He was with an old friend of my cantor dad, a distinguished rabbi with a beard and a black coat and who also had all the answers. They were discussing something like divinity, and the conversation took a left turn into their views on good and evil. They continued to make facile points, using their own words and their indoctrinated brains, and, as they did, I kept thinking, "There ain't no hope, man. There ain't no hope."

To this day, my friend The Colonel says, "A woman's voice should never be heard above a whisper. It's offensive to a man's ear."

I have a woman friend who had been married for twenty-six years and was going through a vicious divorce, negotiating the settlement, children, house, resources, money. Before they finished, the husband had a stroke. He was raced to a hospital. Two hours later, I received a telephone call from the woman. "Thank God my husband died. Now I get everything."

My mind jumps to the family that was grieving over their five-year-old boy, who got run over by a Ford. The family had gotten together to console one another: mother, father, grandparents, cousins, nephews, friends. "We'll see Joey in heaven" was the consensus. "Eventually we'll be together again." Is this innocence or psychosis? This is the world I live in. I think of who I am. My life, my activities, my experiences, my take, and you know what, I tell myself I ain't half bad.

Separate lives enter the picture. I hold on to Elizabeth One. Elizabeth Two. Elizabeth Three. My wife evolves into this complete person. This beautiful person. This kind and generous and self-sacrificing person. But the Elizabeth I started out with is gone. The Elizabeth that needed me desperately was Elizabeth One. This Elizabeth I now call Elizabeth Three. She's independent, capable of taking care of me. This Elizabeth is so together I feel as if I'm on my own. She does not need to be rescued. I would like to say that this Elizabeth is my moral equivalent, but can I say that being me? I take a deep breath and try to pick some winners. Like the old days, I can still pick winners. And Elizabeth and her new life and Liam with his have become what any dad and husband would want for them. Yes it is. So I endure and admire it and become a grandstand manager. That's a term you have to be a baseball junkie to know. It means you have an opinion. It's loud and it's silent, but it is a voice in an empty room. I live each day with friends of a lifetime who no longer call. They're gone! Everything is disappearing, and yet Elizabeth and I are still holding hands and evolving for the better. And now I have this perfect wife who has gone from Elizabeth One to Elizabeth Perfect. She's beautiful, cosmopolitan, talented, productive. Functioning like the brilliant woman that was beneath the surface pain of that first connection. From Kafkaesque to worldly femme. From crawling to leaping. From being all mine to being all here. To being a whole person. A complete person. With generosity, shortcomings, strivings, good days and bad days, and always caring days. And still a great mom and partner and friend and everything I want her to continue to be. A whole person. Amen! Elizabeth One did it. She grew up just fine. I love you, Elizabeth. I love you.

I telephone Elizabeth from our New York residence at four in the morning.

"David, obviously, this getting up at four in the morning to work on your book isn't working. You're disoriented. Maybe you're having a senior moment. Liam never said you were a jerk. Right now, he's having his own issues. He's cramming for American history, chemistry, and math tests. He has to prepare for a robotics competition. He's upset, but not with you, with himself. He wants a girlfriend, and he doesn't have one. He feels terrible about himself. Don't you remember what it is to be a teenager?"

Elizabeth is correct. I must get more sleep. The main thing is my Squirt doesn't think I'm a jerk.

But he would think "jerk" and a whole lot worse if he knew.

Today, New York is in the middle of a monster blizzard. The snow is piling up. Looks like it's going to be anywhere from fifteen to eighteen inches. Sanitation trucks and plows are doing their best, but the city is at a standstill. I go down to the lobby. Barry English is our evening concierge; Gerardo Camacho is the night porter. Both live in Mott Haven. No buses or trains running to or from the Bronx. Conditions are terrible. I'm going to tell these men that Elizabeth is at our house in North Salem. Liam is in Wallingford. They can sleep here. I have plenty of space. Then, I'm going to take one of Elizabeth's Eszopiclone sleeping pills and get a good night's sleep.

I stare at my collages. They are unwieldy, ambiguous, not a crime mystery with cause and effect and plenty of clues. I'm looking at another piece of the puzzle. I use these words loosely, as life is heedless, free spirited, and reeking with mean-spirited absurdity. So why should my collages, within their boundaries, not have imprecise highlights, profligate darkness? They do! I do! Life does!

When I finished the draft of what would be my only bestseller, I was exhausted. Still relatively young, I felt *The Handicapper* was a good book. Somewhat smart, somewhat ready to be read by a sharp eyed editor. I had lunch with Debbie Turner before traveling on the A train down to Urizen Books, in the West Village. It was a small, independent press with a prestigious list of elegant if not mainstream authors. Michael Roloff, the publisher, was a friend of a chum of mine, Susan Braudy, a senior editor at *Ms.* magazine. Roloff was somewhat neurotic. Susan had warned me that he had been unduly intrigued by her tall tales of my gangster connections. Roloff bought into my handicapping mythology as if he were reading *The Godfather*.

He was convinced that he could take my 623 pages and pull off a Mario Puzo.

"I can cut your novel down to 350 pages," he said. "We'll work together. Listen to me—I can take this manuscript and . . . Don't worry, I can come over to your place. We'll work out a time frame that you can live with."

When Roloff came over, he inhaled the blooms on my landscaped terrace. He also must have had a whiff of my novel's potential because he sat down at my desk and for the next five months, slaved with me to accomplish his objective.

"If Urizen thinks your book is that commercial, Davey boy," Solomon told me, "why don't you sell it to one of the mainstream publishers? They have the machinery to do something for you. With Urizen, you have no chance. Tell you what, Davey boy, run with it. If any of the heavyweights bite, buy the book back from Roloff. Whatever he wants will be peanuts. His independent house isn't worth three dinners at my steakhouse—no offense, Davey boy."

Novelists of pedigree by rule never make a dollar, and Michael Roloff's list was saturated with authors of that esoteric ilk. I listened to Solomon. I raced all over the city. I gave eleven estimable publishing houses the same ultimatum. "You have one week to make a decision—that's it! If you don't give me what I'm asking, I'm having Urizen publish my book."

I made a once-in-a-lifetime deal. Ended up with a bestseller. I'm not ashamed. Who doesn't chase the almighty dollar? Deals didn't start with our current president. Guys like me might not know one bottle of French wine from another, but all of America knows that they'd rather read James Patterson than Peter Handke.

But, of course, I would rather Liam know me as a literary artist than as that author of *The Handicapper*. And the money that pays for Choate didn't come from writing that bestseller.

Lately, I've been having this dream. A cleaning lady with a wet mop and a broom enters my living room. She knows her job. Does not need instructions. The room has wet spots on the floor. Dust pools and debris. The cleaning lady's function is to make sure that by the time she leaves, this living space is as squeaky clean as an operating theatre. She vigorously attacks every cobwebbed corner. Mops up all the slush.

When she finishes, there is nothing left outside of a shiny immaculately wax-polished parquet floor. She inspects her work. Nods in approval. Makes the sign of the cross. Bends over and takes a semiautomatic weapon from her shopping bag.

This is where the dream ends. I awake and begin my day.

Not long before Elizabeth asked me about Evan Strome, I awoke with the intention of confessing to her, deed by deed, exactly what transpired during my handicapping years. I was ready to disclose my own brutality, without cowardly deflecting my acts to Solomon Lepidus' primordial behavior. It had seemed like forever in the past, but I had remained mute as to how I had seared my own soul to make money.

Money! That's all it was. I did odious things to make lucre. I not only delegated others to the killing fields, but I personally did heinous things to people, to families, when you extend the harm.

On that winter morning, when Elizabeth opened her eyes and smiled innocently at me, I began to confess. "I'm not even close to the man who you think I am."

I stopped, and the cowardly person inside me took over. I reverted to the craven individual I am. I smoothly moved on to half-truths and tales of lesser villainy.

Elizabeth stared at me. Remained silent. Then she responded in a voice that was almost cheerful. "David. I've never once asked you to confess things concerning your difficult past. The truth is that I don't want you to spell it out to me or to Liam. For me, it's enough that you have an aching heart and carry inside yourself the kind of weighted awareness that knows the difference between the man you are and the man you were. Liam also understands that you are haunted by your past. He too doesn't need for you to spell any of it out. I've spoken about this with him at length. Told him that you have punished yourself for years and years and years." She paused. "Liam understands that you're not perfect. Just yesterday, he told me, 'My Ba is a perfectly imperfect person.'" Elizabeth smiled. "It doesn't detract from either of us loving you." She paused again. "I think since Liam was nine or ten, he's been acutely aware that you aren't anyone's role model. He loves you, David. Yet he has never once said to me that he wants to live his life as you've lived yours."

* * *

Many times, I rationalize away my inexcusable transgressions by convincing myself that my past was lived by someone a great deal less prepared for life than the man I am today. Sometimes I am more philosophical, and I try to reinforce my self-worth by telling myself, "There aren't good people and bad people. There are shades of this and that." But I know this much. At this moment, I'm absorbing Elizabeth and Liam's pure-hearted souls. Breathing a whole lot less laboriously than I ever have before.

I don't want to lose them.

I must write to Liam.

> *Liam Dunn Lazar*
> *Choate Rosemary Hall*
> *336 Christian Street*
> *Wallingford, CT 06492-3800*
>
> *Hi Liam:*
>   *I just want to tell you that you are not me. You're so much better. You're what I want you to be. I don't know if I'm making any sense right now but inside of me, I'm feeling a whole lot cleaner because of you. So, thank you, Liam. I love you Squirt.*

All these years, I've carried a dark secret from those closest to me. Ironically, according to many, my life is glamorous, romantic, adventurous, exciting. It isn't! I was the one who killed a man under the railroad tracks at 117th and Park in the shootout with Champ Holden. I never knew the man's name until the day I ran into Solomon Lepidus' former head of security, Joe Bruno, at Porterhouse in the Time Warner building. He recognized me at once. I didn't know him from the cowboy steak I was chewing.

"I just want to shake your hand," Joe Bruno said. "Not because of all that money you screwed Angelo Ferrari out of. To me, you must've been a genius to be able to pull that off but because of what you did to Frankie Zarilla. I wanted to kill that Guinea prick myself!" Bruno vigorously shook my hand.

I invited him to sit down at our table to have a drink. I was with two retired friends who had been academics at Columbia. They gave me a look like Liam gives me when I start pontificating about my gambling career. When Bruno left, I told my friends that Frankie Zarilla had worked with me, adding "color" to a film script I wrote years ago. Both professors accepted my deceit. Of course, they did. Who in his right mind would believe that Elizabeth's husband, Liam's father, a family man living in the rolling hills of North Salem, could ever have lived the life that I lived? Sometimes even I don't. It's so far-fetched, so over the top, that many times I believe it's better as pretense than it is as a true-life story.

I'm thinking how elated I was a couple of months ago when Liam was going to visit his mother and me for a weekend. He texted, asking if it was all right if he brought a friend. I texted him back,

"No problem."

And now that memory is tainted because those were the same words Joe Bruno used when he told me that Frankie Zarilla was dead.

CHAPTER 15

A new day. I'm at Equinox trying to keep limber when this young woman comes up to me.

"I want to introduce myself. I live in your building. Moved in with my husband last month."

We speak for a while, and then I say, "Why don't you knock on my door? I'm in the penthouse. My rooftop garden is one of a kind."

I'm bragging. My garden overlooks Central Park and is three thousand square feet of plants, shrubs, trees and spring, summer, and fall flowers. It's almost as if you were spending the day at the New York Botanical Gardens.

When the young woman arrives, it doesn't take her long to sit down and tell me that she wanted to meet me because she's an English major and is attempting to write a novel.

Within minutes, I'm the proverbial old man telling her stories from my life.

"I did have my Maxwell Perkins. Michael Roloff. He was the publisher of Urizen Books and a damned good editor. A Peter Handke scholar and a translator, too. He had been responsible for translating several Herman Hesse novels for Farrar, Straus and Giroux. Roloff's list at Urizen was awesome to me. From Sam Shepard to Jean-Paul Sartre. And now he was giving me a contract. My novel went from a 623-page literary disaster to a marketable 372-page book during his watch. I bought the book back from Urizen and sold it two weeks later to Crown. Herb Michaelman, the editor-in-chief at Crown, along with Nat Wartels, the chairman of the Crown Publishing Empire, coerced me into refining the book even further. I ended up with a Book of the Month Club bestseller."

I don't give the young woman the detail that Debbie Turner and I went our separate ways during this time or that when I was on the obligatory twelve-city book tour, TV, media coverage, book signings at what seemed like every bookstore in the country, Debbie wasn't there. What the hell does it all mean when the woman you love isn't there?

My novel made noise. I became a someone. I found myself on Page Six. Of course, over my lifetime, the important money I made came from wagering on college basketball games. Picking winners. FUCK YOU, WORLD! I'M FREE!

I guess I'm sounding as smug as the Emir of Qatar, Sheikh Tamim bin Hamad al Thani, the natural gas billionaire's billionaire, but I'm not.

"FUCK YOU, WORLD! I'M FREE!" I shout to the skies and to the earth and even as I scream this exhilarating cleansing, there is a quiver inside me, more than a tremor. I know that I am not free, that the tumor, this earth, shows us rather quickly that we are commanded by private and public abominations, political, social, metaphysical afflictions that dominate us from birth to death, that there isn't such a thing as freedom, only respite and illusion, our lives are momentary and fragile, that the nonsense that I went through with Leslie Kore was nothing compared to the obscenities I experienced once I chose the world to which I was committed, a world where fifty-three percent in victories was necessary to avoid destruction, that forty-seven percent meant obliteration, that the responsibility I took on would tighten my grip on certitude, the skinny belief that I would not give in to the pitfalls of obsession, distraction, compulsion, recklessness, or emotion. And that's why I now have a more lenient opinion of Leslie Kore and no longer believe she was all wrong, all odious, all unethical, all immoral, as unprincipled as I said she was, that she was just another human being caught up as I was in the ether, and that's where I remain in thought and soul each time I gaze out at Central Park and upper Manhattan, a northern view that during summer nights has a lighted halo around the rim of Yankee Stadium, Central Park West, Fifth Avenue, and during the greenless winter, naked trees in the Great Park, snow dripping out onto Manhattan sidewalks, dented, sun-faded taxicabs, soiled black, brown, yellow and Caucasian people walking dogs, jogging, killing one another, small children scurrying, old people shuffling, younger people going to offices or to some ephemeral everywhere, each one just breathing and dying, and there I would be day after day, on my Manhattan rooftop terrace saying something as inane as FUCK YOU, WORLD! I'M FREE!

* * *

How do I explain what attracted me to men like Solomon Lepidus? To a life that was an about face to the one in which I was weaned. My parents were sober, intelligent people. My mother, warm and bright. She was as decent as—to use my own favorite word—dawn. My father was terrified of his own shadow. As inflexible as a Roman Catholic. He had a soft belly, spindly legs, a pink crown atop his head. He came home every night to his "Pearl." If he saw a woman that he was attracted to, I guarantee you, he averted his eyes, took a deep breath, and started praying. One time, Leslie and I were together in my dad's study. Leslie was sitting on the piano bench in front of my father's Steinway. Leslie was perfect in those days. All allure. Her long, shapely legs were crossed. She started in her deliberate, cruel way to flirt with my father. The cantor's erotic longings were evoked. His erection was obvious. Leslie smiled at my dad. Continued flirting. Finally, my father walked unsteadily out of the room. Went somewhere where he could pray. My mom saw Leslie for who she was. Remained quiet, knowing full well that I was already hooked. Once you're under the spell of that kind of woman, it is what it is. You only extinguish it through disillusionment, pain, or the progression of time. I was hooked for seventeen years. Through Leslie's first two marriages, through our own marriage—in the bathroom, in the shower, in Madison Square Garden, in St. Patrick's Cathedral, where we started kissing but told to leave before things warmed up. At the Metropolitan Opera House—wherever we were. From Checker cabs to the last row of the bleachers at Yankee Stadium, I just never got enough of Leslie Kore. Seventeen years of that woman, and I would've signed up for another seventeen! Thank someone that she screamed, "Get out! Get out! You gambler! You . . ." and all the other invective she threw at me. Of course, Leslie was mostly correct. I was the screw up, not Leslie. She had her truths. I had mine. I also had a whole lot less. Let's call less an accursed muscle that needs to take off and express itself from the inside out. Curse the artistic muscle. It's romantic nonsense in this world of ours. Try makin' a living auditioning for Lear, playin' a horn, bangin' away at a keyboard, or slappin' some paint on a canvas. Just try it. It's a million to one against you! That's one of the reasons I'm always buying winter coats for friends who are trying to make it as actors. Maybe the main reason I'm a helper is that I've never forgotten how brutal it is out there. How impossible.

But back to what made me have such an affinity for Solomon Lepidus.

Solomon Lepidus lived an exciting life. Did things, as Sinatra sang, "My Way." Which of course, was "Solomon's Way." He didn't cower. Didn't buckle. Didn't pray or question. He was nefarious, to be sure. Lethal, callous, brutal, dehumanized for damned sure. But he was also a rejoinder-magnet to a boy who was yearning to break out. Who was looking for something more. Who wanted adventure. An exciting life. Much more than a bar mitzvah or a nine-to-five existence. I've seen too many people genuflecting in synagogues, churches, and mosques, people who were always struggling to support someone else's life. I didn't want that. I never thought about it in those terms, but I knew that I wanted to feel alive. Be alive. Live alive. Love alive. And if it wasn't going to be by making a buck pounding a typewriter and sleeping with Leslie, then well, it might as well be by entering a world of danger. And I think without actually thinking about it, my attraction to an exhilarating, perfidious existence was as much in me as catching a fly ball on the run was to Willie Mays, hitting a baseball was to Ted Williams, or shooting a basketball was to Jerry West, and that's as much as I can figure about why I gravitated to, lived with, yes, went to bed with a man and men on whom most people wouldn't even puke.

I would work through the night, bleary-eyed, until four or five in the morning. Papers spread out all over my desk, on the floor. The information would be classified: records, rosters, match-ups, coaches, scores, stats, tendencies, referees. Everything I could think of was placed and categorized into my "Holy Book." It resulted in me having a winning percentage from 1971 through 2006 of just over sixty-two percent. Only one year did I not win important money.

I know that I am self-aggrandizing. Glorifying my own introspections. Going inside oneself reveals self-absorption excess: ego! In canvassing these years of my life, I glimpse so much of it that has been spent on nothingness rather than on meaningful endeavors. Frequently, I ask how much of me has been used to help make real change. Significant moments are as sporadic as brown leaves in the middle of July. Cigarette butts squashed out in ceramic ashtrays offer more evidence of a sense of intrepid purpose. My own unsettling forays to find dignity and authenticity were and are weak and inadvertent. Am I any different from so many of my contemporaries? Is this the best I can do? I know the answer. It's in my belly. It does not comfort me to realize that people are doing the same right now. So many of us screw up. Waste so much of our lives. Whenever I visit my son's privileged school, talk to his teachers about how he is doing with his math, chemistry, or French, or his dalliances with mime or robotics, I always think to myself that Choate should be teaching something more than what is being taught. Something more to African Americans being shot. Police officers being killed. Women being raped. Muslims being Hitlerized. I've disappointed myself. Failed myself. Today is a bad day. I'm biting my lower lip. Blood is oozing. There was a death. Someone extremely close to me has died. Robin Wicks Romano.

Robin passed last month. I volunteered to give a eulogy at Campbell Brothers Funeral Home on Madison Avenue. It was heartfelt. Everything I said—from the first night we met at the Spindletop in 1958—I truly meant. I did leave out one thing that always annoyed me about Robin: whenever I invited her to dinner, she'd say, "Let me text my daughter. She gets out of work about now. Maybe she can join us."

Invariably, Robin took advantage of me like that. That wouldn't have been so bad. I liked Robin's daughter. But what I didn't appreciate was that her daughter always made sure to order two of everything. "My husband's going to love this food."

I look at my two collages. More X'd out friends than ever before! Who's left for me to have dinner with? To go to ballgames with? Watch football with on Sundays? Debate about who was the best—Michael, LeBron, Kobe, Magic, or The Big O? All gone. And who has replaced them? What has replaced them? The president's brand of nationalism—hard-edged nationalism with its gut level cultural appraisals and hardline stances on trade and immigration. A nation reeling over sexual misconduct. What happened to me? I once marched in Selma. Wrote a book on the black/white problems in America. Today—would I be worrying about Latoya Earl or her son, Tommy? I don't think so. I don't mean because of my age. I mean, today, I probably would be taking an entry-level position on Wall Street or using my family's contacts to get into some insatiable hedge fund or high-tech start-up or some scarlet white-shoe law firm . . . or even worse than that—giving in or giving up the fight. Today, people are either bland or extreme. I am bland. I am extreme. I am filled with myself ME . . . ME . . . ME . . . ME. Are greed and Amazon and Apple and Microsoft and Facebook and the other mushrooming mega-companies and one percenter electronic visions of free market capitalism while giving up our inner life, grievances, and consciences all that we have left? I'm spewing thoughts that have been waiting to be puked out for far too many years. Maybe it's because of a lifetime of about-facing, wrong-doing. That book that I wrote when I was married to Leslie—*American Racism*, the one over which she hissed, "Nigger lover!" at me whenever she peeked over my shoulder. The major conflict that we had, that started me on those hate-fucks. Is that who I am? Anal leakage. Ineluctable truths.

I'm remembering a donnybrook I had with Elizabeth. "You're not LBJ," she said. "You might be complex. You might even be contradictory but that doesn't make you LBJ!"

We had been discussing different presidents, and I said that Lyndon Johnson might be my all-time MVP.

"It was Johnson, Liz, who signed the Civil Rights Act of 1964."

"It was President Johnson, David, who earlier in his career spoke against civil rights."

"It was Johnson who declared unconditional war against poverty."

"David," Elizabeth countered, "it was President Johnson who escalated the war in Vietnam."

I was trying to make a point with Elizabeth that even American presidents are complex and contradictory. Not just me.

Solomon Lepidus, too, was complex, conflicted, blood soaked; a maze, like so many of us. He was my closest friend, never my enemy. I learned from him. Things that I didn't—couldn't—learn in books. Things like staking hundreds of people to holiday turkeys, start-up money. I try to do things like that too, but I'm no match for Solomon. He liked people. Helped as many as twenty-five a day. That's about how many people with money problems would call his office each day. And Solomon would listen.

"Don't worry, Allie boy. That's not a problem at all. The only problem I can't help you with is the one that's terminal." He'd end each of his conversations with, "Just keep me even," or "Take it easy."

One of his most exciting ventures was producing the first million-dollar musical on Broadway, and Solomon Lepidus knew as much about theater as Forrest Gump! Yet, when his musical went down, he walked through the stage door, planted himself on the main stage, gathered all the actors and the crew around him, and said, "I just want to thank you. Never had so much fun in all my life. All of you are invited to my restaurant whenever you want, and if any of you have trouble finding jobs, don't hesitate to call my office."

Solomon was a godsend to so many people that he should've run for mayor. I would have to say that aside from my wife Elizabeth and son Liam, both of whom weren't around until well after Solomon Lepidus passed, the most impressive thing about my life had little to do with the books I've written, the women I've loved, or my handicapping. The most special thing was having the good fortune to have known that five-foot-six-inch, barrel-chested phenomenon. Solomon Lepidus was a New York original.

I was at Solomon's steakhouse one very cold Tuesday night during the second week of December 1973. It was just about eighteen months after I had taken my book cartons and moved out of my parents' home. I had made $109,000 *tax free* that year. I had become a someone. I felt good about myself. And now I was expanding. I was taking in partners, and, thanks to The Colonel, guys were coming out of the woodwork.

"David Lazar is the greatest handicapper since . . . " he would tell everyone. Legitimate businessmen and wise guys alike would proposition me. Begging me to give them my games and offering me deals. That's when Nathan Rubin first came in.

"Ya see, sonny boy, this is the way I do things. I put up two thirds of the money. You put up one third. I don't want to hear what your deal with Solomon Lepidus is. Lepidus is a sucker. You want my money? My outs? My information? You do it my way."

There wasn't much of a crowd in Solomon's steakhouse that night. A winter blizzard had hit the city. Hardly anyone showed up. I had Solomon all to myself.

"Davey boy, I'm going to join my wife and daughter this weekend in London. If you find a special game, don't worry about calling me. You know how much I hate to talk on phones!"

"Solomon, I feel uncomfortable betting this kind of money when you don't have a clue as to what's going on. Why can't you do what Nathan Rubin does? Check in with me every night before the games begin."

"What the hell, Davey boy! Don't be such a businessman! I trust you." Solomon gave me one of his broad grins. "What the hell, Davey boy! It's only money! Just keep pickin' winners!"

Solomon Lepidus was a primordial man with simple truths. I don't say this to denigrate Solomon; it was just how he lived and thought. "Davey boy, first you make your money; then you live your life," he said the first time we met. I had my nose in Jean-Paul Sartre's *Being and Nothingness*. I thought Solomon was aboriginal.

In 1985 Solomon told me, "There's this new telemarketing company in Canada. They have a once-in-a-lifetime idea. They need money to expand. That's me, Davey boy. I'm buying fifty-one percent of the company with the six million I still have left."

"Don't be crazy, Solomon!"

"I'm going to take a shot, Davey boy. I have to. Otherwise, my employees are without jobs. They're mostly family men; they need their jobs."

"Take your six million and run. You can still have a great life—you're not dead!"

"I have obligations, Davey boy. People are counting on me."

In the middle of the winter of 1986, Amy Cho and I were having dinner at Dewey Wong's. I had a brown paper bag with $37,000 in Franklins to give to Solomon. He was over two hours late. Finally, at 10:05, he arrived. Before reaching our table, he stopped to say hello to half a dozen people who recognized him. One of them was Bobby Murcer. Another was Abe Beame, the first Jewish mayor of New York. Possibly the most ineffectual, too. According to Solomon, "He was a clubhouse Democrat, Davey boy. The city's budget chief who during the seventies because of some influence from some politicians with clout, if you know what I'm saying, ended up mayor and presided over the largest budget crisis in New York City history. It might not have been Abe Beame's fault, but it certainly was his undoing. He should've stayed at Richmond Hill High School as a teacher. That was the best job he ever had, he usta tell me." Another was a Brooklyn D.A. Solomon shook his hand, patted him on the back, whispered confidences. Both men laughed so hard that they started crying. When Solomon finally reached our table, he didn't greet me with his usual,

"What's doin', Davey boy?" Instead, it was with a terrible shaking of his head, his raspy voice quavering. "I don't know what's wrong with me, Davey boy."

Amy began to sob.

"I don't know what's wrong with me, Davey boy. I just blew $90,000 in Atlantic City. Had to sign an IOU. I'm crazy." Solomon shook his head. "I can't afford it. I know that better than anyone." I was earning major dollars that winter. I was on a real roll and handing over wads of Franklins every week to Solomon so he could meet his payroll.

Amy cried herself to sleep that night. She loved Solomon. Solomon helped her start her jewelry business. Supplied her with all the silver and gold that she needed. Gave her advice. Sat her down and told her step-by-step what to do.

"Amy girl, remember this, the best place to look for a helping hand is at the end of your own right arm. Make this happen, Amy girl! Give it everything you've got."

"I will, Mr. Lepidus. I swear."

The college hoops season ended. There were no more five-star bets. Besides, my incredible winning streak had ended. I am not self-defeating. I continued to help Solomon. As the Greek philosophers would say, "In moderation . . . "

The incredible percentage of winning that I achieved over a lifetime didn't come easy. There wasn't one day that the strong and the weak in me wasn't tested. There wasn't a day that inside that erratic mind of mine, I wasn't on the verge of walking away. Each loss killed me. Every time I had to get a score, whether it would be at halftime, during the last two minutes of a game, hell, even during the first five minutes, I held my breath, clenched my talisman silver dollar, and died a little. Thirty-plus years of dying. Thirty-plus years of being under the gun. And then those contracts on my head, that too, unnerved me; I paid a price for the life I led. All that winter, I picked nothing but winners. I had won something like twenty-nine of the first thirty-seven games that I wagered on that season.

Besides the hard work, the long hours, the anxiety, the danger, the damage to my soul, I had to tap into the art of handicapping. I found the gestalt of handicapping, which, besides odds, and home court advantage, and good coaching and numbers, and all the other details, demanded an intuition, a sense of where the whole was greater than the sum of its parts. And I learned to trust it, when to put down a bet and when not to. It was a gift, but I earned it.

In 1986, I was as well-heeled as a one percenter. Solomon Lepidus being more than a great man to me, I could never say no to him. Of course, during my handicapping career, Solomon Lepidus had saved my life, too. Right now, I think of riding in a Lincoln town car with the buttons going down for one of those end-of-life rides. One phone call was all I had left.

"Solomon, I got a problem . . ."

There were five or six other crises like that when my life depended on Solomon Lepidus. And each time he came through.

But Solomon also disappointed me.

When he was negotiating to buy the New York Yankees: "Davey boy, I promise you, if I get to own the Yankees, you're going to be my general manager."

Solomon changed his tune when the negotiations became serious.

"I'm sorry, Davey boy. I think Jackie Robinson's the right man for the job."

If Solomon Lepidus sounds larger than life, it's only because he was larger than life. I, too, would have selected Jackie Robinson to manage my team. In fact, the day Solomon told me about his change of mind to Jackie Robinson was Debbie Turner's twenty-fourth birthday, October 11, 1972. The four of us were driving to Solomon's steakhouse for dinner.

"Mr. Robinson," I asked, "how did you ever find the courage to stand up to those beanballs that those racists were throwing at your head?"

Jackie Robinson looked me straight in the eye, "I guess God gave me big shoulders," he said.

CHAPTER 16

I'm gazing at my two collages. Recalling a thousand memories. Rodney Parker grew up in Bed-Stuy. Never graduated the fifth grade. I met him when I was an undergrad at NYU. We were both seventeen. Rodney was shining shoes in front of the old Madison Square Garden. I had an extra ticket, which I gave to him. He said he'd meet me inside the Garden. He never showed. The following week, I was again going to the Garden for an NYU game and saw Rodney in front of Nedick's scalping tickets.

"You gave me a profession, man!" he yelled.

We became friends, remained friends for fifty-seven years. Rodney died five years ago. His scalping did a whole lot of good. Eight children and all with decent lives and college educations. This feel-good story hasn't even begun to tap the surface of all that Rodney Parker did. He saved more young men from the streets than anyone I knew. Through the years, he kick-started hundreds of basketball careers. Got boys into Five-Star Camps, junior colleges, Division One colleges, even the NBA. Rodney ended up knowing just about everyone in the game. The only negative to the story is that every year I write a letter trying to get Rodney Parker into the New York Basketball Hall of Fame, and every year, the board members reject my plea. They say Parker made his living scalping tickets and stick their collective noses up in the air. Rodney Parker wasn't just one of my closest friends, he was a New York prototype. Besides helping all those youngsters, he did other things. But no one is a saint. In Rodney's case, he made serious moves on all the women I had ever loved, but that's another story.

I wrote my novels, picked my games, had my relationships. It wasn't romantic love all the time. Here's a snapshot of a woman I knew in 1979 who was a centerfold in one of those girlie magazines.

"David, that's pathetic!" I can hear Elizabeth complain.

Here's one of Whitey Reynolds. Hadn't spoken to Whitey Reynolds since we were in high school. He played in the same backcourt as Noah

Weldon back then. Whitey and I were close. We hung out together. Then we lost track of one another. Joya Weldon phoned me two weeks ago to tell me that Whitey's wife had passed. That I should give him a call. When I did, he was still grieving. Of course, he was. What did I expect? The thing is Whitey and I started talking. It was as if we were back at Commerce High School. I didn't invite Whitey to have dinner with me. I thought it was a bit too early for that. Something he said to me made me sad. I mean, outside of the fact that his wife had passed. He said that he never made it. That he tried.

"My dream was to own a diner, Lazar. I ended up a dishwasher. I saw you more than once at the restaurant I worked at."

At eighty, there isn't much left of me. I must remember to tell Elizabeth to pick up a more secure rubber mat for our bathtub. The current one is dangerous. I had safety bars installed in the tub, and it still took me six minutes to climb out. I'm becoming feebler every week. And that's with going to Equinox four times a week and working out with a personal trainer. Maggie Giddens is doing her job. It's me. I never thought I'd be one of these old people. I am. It happens to everyone. Stick around long enough and it's sure to happen. I'm super grateful for these years I've had with Elizabeth. As for friends, at last count, only six of my forty-one closest ones are left. There are several new individuals in my life. When I think of it, ninety percent of my old friends were self-made men and women. Idiosyncratic, with large egos, and that's something that's missing nowadays. I dwell on all my buddies who are gone, from Rodney Parker to Solomon Lepidus to The Colonel.

So many friends gone. The scarce few that are left are in wheelchairs. Have home attendants. Joya Weldon, it seems, is forever going for chemo. Stanley Banks was probably my oldest friend. When I think of what Duke did not do with his life, my mind jumps to Rodney Parker and what he did with his. As for Noah Weldon, he's still my closest friend. For years and years, once a month, we'd have dinner at Sylvia's in Harlem or go down to Little Italy and pig out.

This is sad. Noah doesn't remember he's my closest friend. A stroke unceremoniously dumped him on an anthill in a debris-ridden park in Jamaica, Queens.

Last week I visited Noah in the hospital. He's in bed doing a lot of stammering. Yet he's talking on the phone sounding alert. In fact, so feisty on the phone that he sounds just like he did in 1965 when he took Tommy—Latoya Earl's boy—under his wing. I had talked to Noah about Tommy, and he introduced him to some community leaders in Queens. Didn't stop working with Tommy Earl until he found a concrete way for him to make a living. Now, here I am visiting my best friend since we were fourteen, and Noah is stammering to some woman named Heather Feshbach.

"Don't abandon us like your mother did. The congresswoman gave up on our community. She'd rather make a buck and be a hotshot than do something for people. You know what I told your mother to do with her electoral politics. You've got to stay right here and teach, Heather. Continue teaching and working for the people in your neighborhood. If young people would just do that, the rest of it will take care of itself."

Noah's tirade ended right there. Those were his last words.

Five days went by before I took an Uber up to the Bronxwood Funeral Home. When I got there, I spent some time with Joya. Actually, it wasn't Joya, it was a diminutive, frail, white-haired old woman who I didn't recognize. A stranger in form, but as morally strong and powerful as her voice that cried out to me, "My baby is gone! My baby is gone!" Sixty years of being happily married will do that, I guess.

"My baby is gone!"

I spoke to Noah's son, Jesse, then I was introduced to Noah's grandson, seventeen-year-old Jordan Weldon. Jordan Weldon moved me as much as Noah did the first time we met. He had Noah's effusive smile, his high brow, his warm voice, his good looks. The boy was a reed, well over six feet tall.

"My poppy spoke about you all the time, Mr. Lazar. He said that you were the one white man he trusted." I didn't have to hear any more. That said it all. At the funeral of the 500 or 600 mourners, no more than three or four were Caucasian. The mayor was one of them.

"What a world we live in." Noah would always sigh when we were so very young and trying to change the world.

"My poppy and I were real close, Mr. Lazar. Every Sunday we would sit together at church. No, he never mentioned that he was an All-City basketball player. No! He never mentioned that he played college ball. No! He never mentioned that he was invited to the White House by the

Clintons. My grandma told me about that. No, he never mentioned that you dedicated your first novel to him or that you were the best man at his wedding. No! No! No! But he did tell me all the time about how much work still needed to be done for people. He was a hands-on community leader, Mr. Lazar. My poppy worked with everyone from the mayor to gang leaders to neighborhood people. He knew every church, mosque, and synagogue all throughout Queens. My poppy got along with everyone, Mr. Lazar. He drilled into me two things that he made me scribble on my wall. One: People are important. Two: Read! Read! Read!"

Jordan was the spitting image of Noah. It was eerie at first. I had flashbacks of my first day in Mrs. Martin's homeroom. Noah and I sitting side-by-side and becoming friends.

"I'm going to Howard, Mr. Lazar. I just found out that the school accepted me. After college, I know what I want to do. I'm going to be a civil rights lawyer and work for people. Try and do the same kind of things my poppy did. I mean every day—" Jordan hesitated and then stammered, "My poppy was a great man, Mr. Lazar. I loved him so much!" He started to sob.

"I loved your grandfather from the time we were fourteen, Jordan." I said, putting my arm around his shoulder. Inside I felt very much as I did as a fourteen-year-old when Noah and I first met. I felt so much better.

Two weeks later, I was still thinking of Noah and Joya . . . When I think of Joya, it's as a fifteen-year-old with bruised plum-colored cheeks, a Booster's white sweater, green skirt, knee socks, running out on the basketball court to cheer for Commerce and, of course, Noah. Joya Highsmith was so damn young. So darn adorable. So full of life. She was the feistiest girl at Commerce. Joya bossed Noah around from the first day they met. "Hey, Weldon," she would snap. "I'm here. Stop ogling them women." Noah would freeze, take orders, do what he was told. Even at sixteen, he knew who the boss was and he also knew he loved Joya.

When I saw Joya at the funeral she was not someone I was familiar with. She had shrunk to the size of a tiny lady; a kind of elderly citizen, frail, ghostly, and slow of pace. She had white, white hair that was thinning in the front, tightly pulled back to cover the bald patches at the top of her head. Her forehead was the most prominent part of her. It was pulsating, that is, the vein in the middle was. Her skin was colorless, the rest of her was covered by a gunnysack dress that some might say was smart and stylish. Joya's demeanor was antithetical to the Commerce Booster as my life is different as an octogenarian from my high school days. Yet, Joya's voice hadn't changed at all. She still sounded as alive as sixty years before, no, make that sixty-five. It wasn't Proustian time, but it was a flashback that seemed as if we were back to the you-know-what-can-never-be. Joya's tone, pitch, resonance, social concerns, devotion were all there, the caring qualities, not only for Noah, but for our country.

"Character, that's what's missing in these guys—character! It all starts there." Then Joya fused teardrops into communication. "My baby," must have been repeated as much as "Noah was great. Not only as a husband, Dave, but as a man. Forget the stupid basketball for a minute, do you have any idea how much he did for the people. People!" she said.

"Do you remember when we double-dated with Sheila Tronn?" I asked. We must have been sixteen, maybe seventeen and eighteen. Sheila was fifteen. Redhead and as pretty as a young Rhonda Fleming. For those of you who aren't familiar . . . Rhonda Fleming was an actress.

"Whatever happened to Sheila?" Joya asked. And that started more words, more memories, and then, of course, it was back to my best friend, Noah.

"Noah was more a brother than a friend to me, Joya."

"I know that," she said. "He loved you too."

Do memories remain till our last breaths? Memories, breaths of yesteryear with the oxygen to sustain. Like climbing a ladder till you reach the top step, and then some of us jump. What is left? I asked myself when we completed our connectedness.

So many gone. I mean friends of a lifetime. Guys who never tweeted even once in their entire lives. Some of my friends have still never even heard of iPhones. Men with whom I've laughed and cried. Went all the way to somewhere with. Some of these guys went to the top of their professions. Some to the bottom. We shared lives. Were there for one another. Some of us raised families; some didn't.

"I'm thinking of having another child, Dave," Stickers said.

I had just handed him the money to pay the three months back rent that he owed. He was over seventy by then.

Now I'm thinking of Morty Lefko, The Colonel. He's gone, too. So is Rodney Parker. He's the friend I miss the most. The only one who knew all the women in my life.

"Jessica was the sweetest, Broadway. She made me feel like June was bustin' out all over. Leslie. She was as cold as frost, but she had everything else. Debbie Turner was hard to figure. One day she was a swan in a pond; then next a vulture scavenging for its dinner. Amy. She was always in her own world."

Unfortunately, Rodney Parker never got to know Elizabeth. By the time Liz came into my life, Rodney was closing in on death in a senior citizen's facility. But here's who Rodney Parker was. He bought McDonald's burgers, milkshakes, and Nike shoes for his Playground Prodigies and preached, "Don't ever take drugs! Don't go out with bad women! And don't—and I mean never—hang out on the street after ten!"

Rodney had seen so much violence growing up in Bed-Stuy. He helped boys reach their dreams; he saved lives. Hundreds of them.

Not everything I'm recollecting is from yesterday.

Today, I'm walking to the TDF window on 47th Street to purchase a matinee ticket. It's a whole lot cheaper than paying full price at the box office.

I stop in the middle of the street. Right in the slush and puddles. There are snowdrifts on the curb. I hear, "Mr. Lazar . . . Mr. Lazar."

I turn around. It's Norma Meyers. I worked with her at Welfare.

"How you doin', Mr. Lazar?"

Before I can get in a word, Norma's telling me, "My husband used to be so lively. Now he sits home all the time."

I tell Norma that I didn't recognize her without her Afro. "I cut it, and I'm not dyeing my hair any longer."

Norma starts telling me about the old crew. "Sue Bethel died, and so did Carolyn Shipp. Remember how much Mrs. Shipp loved you? And then there's Mattie Mixon and Joan Pryor. Remember when all of us went to see Joanie in that Van Peebles musical? And did you hear about John Ryan? He moved to Montana when he retired."

Norma shook her head. "That man was always reeking of alcohol and sporting red, watery eyes. And how is Mr. Stiloski? Do you keep in touch with him?"

"'Big John' lives in Tarrytown. He got lucky, Norma. 'Big John' has a fabulous wife."

Stiloski played football at Notre Dame in the fifties. He's dead weight now. Can't walk without the aid of two canes and his wife, Annette. But his voice hasn't changed.

"I still speak to 'Big John' every now and then, Norma. And he never fails to call me on my birthday. He's the one guy from our unit that I'm still in touch with."

Norma Meyers rattles off another football team of dead people. People who once had real lives, dignity, clocked in every morning to do something useful, earned a paycheck. While Norma is rattling away, I'm thinking that my time is just around the corner. And then she says, "Do you ever hear from that pretty young girl, Debbie Turner?"

"Never!" I tell Norma. Still, after all these years, it's like a dagger going through my gut.

I lied to Norma Meyers. I had heard from Debbie Turner. I recently received a letter from her on fancy stationery.

"With my husband, I feel like an equal; with you, I always felt as if you were looking down on me. And when you weren't handicapping or watching ballgames or at Solomon's restaurant with your horrible friends, you were writing nine hours a day. And when you weren't doing those things, you still were only involved with yourself. I admit that you've done a whole lot of big things with your life, David, but it's the smaller things that make a relationship work."

Today I visited Ron Nevins at Presbyterian Hospital on 220th Street and Broadway. The Uber drove straight up the steep incline, more like a hill, to the front entrance. I stepped out of the car and drew a deep breath.

When I entered his hospital room, he was still in a deep coma. I took out from of my shoulder bag Shusaka Endo's novel *Silence* and started to read, "Like sand flowing through an hour glass, each day here passed quietly by, my feelings formerly tense and taut like iron now gradually relaxed . . . "

Nothing was left of Ron Nevins. Blind, speechless, lifeless for the past nine days. Before he was transferred to Presbyterian, purely by chance, a friend of mine who was one of Ron's neurosurgeons at Mt. Sinai, told me, "Don't worry about your pal I'm sure he's going to be just fine."

He alleviated some of the pressure on Ron's brain, but it didn't change a thing.

Ron's son Jake, my godson, enters the hospital room. He's taking it hard. He can't let his father go, but he must. The Presbyterian Hospital social workers are compassionate. They're trying to give my godson sufficient time to make the ultimate decision. "It's been nine days . . ." I hear one of the hospital administrators conspiratorially whisper to a social worker.

I tell Jake, "It's your decision. Take your time. You've got to be ready."

At my age, your life is reduced to stories, and that's what I tell Jake. Stories! Stories that his dad and I lived and experienced.

"Here's one about a woman I met back in the day. Her name was Julie Rizzo.

"At midnight, Julie knocked on my door.

"'My boyfriend is in the lobby. He's afraid to come up. He doesn't have the money he owes you.'

"I invited Julie to my rooftop terrace.

"'Wow!' she exclaimed.

"Did you ever hear of Joe DiMaggio? I asked her.

"'Yeah. Sure. He was a baseball player.'

"Joe DiMaggio was famous for his fifty-six-game hitting streak. And in your own way, Julie, you're breaking a streak, too.

"'What's that?' she said and chomped down on her bubble gum.

"You're the first woman up here after midnight with whom I'm not going to bed.

"Julie laughed. It broke the ice."

"Tell me about Solomon Lepidus," Jake said.

"I once had a really bad year. Of the seven men I took in as limited partners, only six made money. The seventh was Solomon. He told me, 'It's not you, Davey boy. It's me. I'm a jinx.'

"Jake, Solomon lost over $200,000 on my college selections that year. I reimbursed him for every cent he lost. It was simple enough. I walked into his office with two brown paper bags and dumped the cash on his desk. Solomon looked up.

"'What's this for?' he asked.

"'It's what you lost with me this season.

'Oh,' he said and that ended the conversation."

I didn't tell Jake that Solomon always kept Chapter Eleven papers in his desk drawer. If Solomon didn't want to help you, he would open his drawer and confide, as if he were a father talking to his son, "No one knows this, buddy boy, but I've been forced to declare bankruptcy." Everyone's best friend would shake his head and take your hand. "I just can't help anyone, anymore."

My godson winced. Minutes later, he was asking about *The Tutor*, one of my early creations that his dad always favored.

"I couldn't blame John Farrar for my book not getting published, Jake. He prepared me. As soon as I walked into his office that day, the first thing he told me was, 'Young man, are you aware that we receive upwards of 2,400 manuscripts a year from unpublished novelists. At the most, we publish maybe three or four of them.'"

Jake and I sat in Ron Nevins' hospital room for four days. Never did I run out of stories. Never did Jake ask me to stop. By the fourth day, Jake was making contributions on his own.

"My dad was a great admirer of Ulysses S. Grant. When I was little, he would tell me almost every night what the general had told his own son, 'In order to win respect, never deceive nor play an artificial part. Simply be yourself.'"

My godson told me several things I didn't know. I listened. Continued to contribute my own stories.

"I met Lincoln Kirstein through your dad, Jake. When Kirstein strolled the city center, with his hands clenched behind his back in his wrinkled, blue serge coat, grimacing, his scowl was both menacing and perturbed. The leggy dancers blanched. Ron and I were seeing several of those long-legged ballerinas for lunch or dinner. Sometimes more.

"But it was Lincoln Kirstein who was actually Mr. More. He was the founder of the New York City Ballet. He had accomplished the impossible dream of giving George Balanchine the keys to the kingdom. The Russian was one hell of a choreographer, but, in my opinion, the ballet company itself was Kirstein's vision. My impression was that George Balanchine would have been just as content choreographing for a pick-up troupe. Balanchine was more like a pure-hearted writer. Give a dedicated novelist a Remington, and he's just going to tap those keys.

"Similarly, give Balanchine a hardwood floor and a dancer or two and he's going to choreograph. As for Lincoln Kirstein, he was chronically agitated, obviously bipolar, and had little if any self-control. Librium was not around back then, and Kirstein was the mortal enemy of me and your father, too. Both of us would bring flowers—the most extravagant and beautiful bouquets possible—to the company's female dancers. Your dad, of course, picked up the tab. Unfortunately, Kirstein would snap disapprovingly, 'Girls! Girls! This is a workplace, not a boudoir!'

"Here's one story, Jake, that I've never told anyone. Your father and I were having dinner one evening at Cafe des Artistes with Janet Gretchler. Janet was a Balanchine dancer. Edward Villella, who was sitting at a table in a far corner, spotted Janet and rushed over. As he was doing so, George Balanchine enters the restaurant. When he notices Villella, he too rushes over. He asks your father if he can sit with us. Of course, your dad says, 'Yes.' You can only imagine how Ron was beaming, Jake. It was a glorious moment for him. For me, I sort of took things like that in stride. Anyway, here's your father chatting and dining with Mr. B and Edward Villella. Your dad was great at playing that kind of role, Jake. He had panache. He thrived in that kind of scene. His dress was always impeccable. Your father always wore a bow tie with one of his classy Brioni or Scali or Jacques Denoyer suits. I usually had on a Balmain or a James Carroll sports coat. And I always made sure to wear Alexander Shields shirts and ties. Got to admit, Jake, both of us were sort of impressive in those days. Not only our wardrobes, but both of us were good looking.

"Of course, the reason I had such a great wardrobe and looked so good was strictly because of your dad. Your father taught me how to dress. Where to go for razor cuts. How to hold a knife and fork. And so much more. Believe me, Jake, just in case you aren't fully aware of it, it was your father who picked up the tab for everything back in those day. And I mean everything. Anyway, George Balanchine had this weird habit of naming his dancers after animals. He didn't know your father or me outside of the two or three times we shook hands at one of Kirstein's fundraisers. And now, here we are sitting with Mr. B. and I suddenly notice that he's staring at the two of us.

"And he keeps staring. I guess you could say, if you want to be polite, that Mr. B. was an observer of people. To me he was staring. Suddenly, he stops staring. 'I'm going to call you "Fox," he tells me. And you, Mr. Nevins, are "Sparrow."'

"Let me tell you, Jake, that might've been the highlight of your dad's life. For the remainder of that year, your dad insisted that I address him as 'Sparrow.'"

Ron Nevins didn't do much with his eighty-one years. The second half of his life was a disaster. The most he did was go to temple, genuflect to his god. For years and years, I would tell Ron, "Make a New Year's resolution to do something different this year. I don't care if it's getting rid of your toupee or becoming a Roman Catholic. Just do something that will make you feel better about yourself."

"The same goes for you, Broadway." For years and years, he would advise, "There's a life out there with a loving woman, Broadway. You can still raise a family. Have children. Walk away from the world you're in."

"I never believed in fairy tales," I would tell him.

Ron Nevins worked for the same brokerage firm after he sold his father's sportswear company in 1968. He became the confidante of many a little old lady, assisting them with their portfolios, singing out, "Isn't Rebecca beautiful?" in internalized tones, about his lacerating wife, struggling to maintain an irresponsible lifestyle, eking out a static salary, piling up debt and more debt, each year.

"Broadway, what do you think of this idea? At Fieldston and Dartmouth I had many, many great friends. I'm still in touch with some of them. I was thinking of drafting a letter. Advising them of my financial situation. Asking each one to contribute $2,000. It would mean very little to these men. Everything to me."

"Don't humiliate yourself, Ron. I'll give you whatever it is you need. Just don't waste the money on a trip to Tahiti or by going to Le Cirque or by buying ABT tickets. Oh, what the hell! Do whatever you like with the money! You deserve better than that from me."

By the time Ron was fifty-five, he was completely dependent upon me. I paid for Jake to go to Ethical Culture. To Fieldston. From there to college. I was the one who beseeched Rebecca, "Do you think it's possible to pay me back at least a small amount of what Ron owes me? Both of you are now working."

"How dare you? How could you ask that?" And the phone went click.

Why did I ask? Stupid! That's why.

As Solomon Lepidus advised, "When you give someone money, Davey boy, it's not a loan; it's a gift."

End time for Ron Nevins. The hospital administrators met with my godson. "Polite" pressure was applied. Jake gave them a nod, a balled fist, tears. I care about my godson. I feel for him deeply. He's sacrificed his own life for the past eight years to take care of his parents. His mother didn't pass until last year. Alzheimer's. Now, I'm telling Jake, "You have to find the strength to move on. The only thing that helps is time." I couldn't stop myself from adding, "Your father should have pushed you out the door. He was selfish."

Ron Nevins told his son, "Follow your religion. Say your prayers. If you run into a problem, talk to the rabbi. But don't worry, Jake. You'll never have money problems. I'm leaving you everything I have."

I'm happy I was able to help Ron and, of course, Solomon. And without handicapping, without all that entailed, I wouldn't have been able to help either or live the life I do.

CHAPTER 17

I'm thinking how great the 1976 college basketball season was for me. I was picking nothing but winners, and a great deal of it was because of Bobby Knight. So, here's a belated thank you to the retired coach. Yes, Coach Knight is my all-time number one coach. He did it when he was in his mid-twenties with the brawny Mike Silliman playing the center position at Army, and, after that, he did it with maybe at the most, a half dozen legitimate McDonald's All-Americans through his fabulous career.

Enough about that kind of romantic nonsense. In 1976, "the General" won the NCAA basketball championship coaching at Indiana. Knight's team won every game in the tournament by the points. I had made sure that Solomon and I parlayed the entire run.

"Just stay with Indiana, Solomon. They're going to cover every game."

It might have been the one time Solomon Lepidus followed my advice. That year, he won enough money on my handicapping to lose $2 million in Las Vegas later that year. Of course, I prospered too. After Knight won the championship, I stepped out on my rooftop and shouted, "Fuck you world! I'm free!"

I think it was the first time, but don't trust me on that.

That same week I drove to Parksville, New York. I had a pick and shovel and maybe a dozen industrial-size black bags filled with Franklins. I buried them under a large elm tree. Scratched into the elm's trunk FUWIF.

Those black bags are no longer buried in Parksville. I had to hand them over to the RICO people. That was another time Solomon saved my ass.

"Now, Davey boy. Tell me the problem you're having with those RICO people."

"Two of them showed up at midnight. They took me downtown. I had to come up with $70,000 just to go home. They had me on tape calling in five dime bets to Angelo Ferrari's office. The irony is they caught me because Giuliani's DA had been investigating Ferrari and had his office phones tapped. Once they started investigating me, they discovered checks I wrote for Amy Cho to Ron Nevins' brokerage firm. I know you always warned me not to leave a paper trail, but I wanted Amy to feel independent. Now, the DA's office is looking into my taxes."

"Don't worry anymore about it. I'll make a few calls. But, Davey boy, I can't get you back that seventy large."

I still have a hell of a lot more bags buried all over the Audubon Trails in Westchester County, and once in a while I still like to step out onto my rooftop and shout, "Fuck you world! I'm free!"

Last week, I drove up to Chappaqua. The trees were barren. Most of the leaves were piling up on dank ground. I brought a pick and shovel. I dug up a dozen black bags. Pretty damn good for a guy who started with a $25 bet. I tore up the ground. I needed to reimburse myself. Replenish my cash flow. Besides, before I know it, Squirt will be moving on to college. And that costs Franklins.

Today there's something on my mind, even more so than when I first read it in 2014. Elizabeth had left me a note on the kitchen table when I returned to our North Salem home.

> *Our first year together I was still recovering from a double mastectomy. I was in desperate need of all that you provided. You extended yourself in a million ways, and if not a passionate lover, then you were a tender one. Our sex life has always been from you to me. After our first two years together, I gradually withdrew. Yet, there has never been any silences or big gaps between us. You were growing older day by day. I was becoming more and more terrified. I don't think you've ever noticed any of this. That feeling of dread that to this day keeps building inside of me. That's why I kept pushing you away. I've been seeing a counselor. That's where I am at this moment. He's helping. Bear with me, David. We have an amiable friendship. A companionable existence. Liam is a great son. It's more than enough for me. But inside, I live in a constant state of fear. There isn't*

*a second that goes by that deep inside, my mind isn't
occupied with your dying.*

That letter has never been discussed. Not once.

I remember women as if it were yesterday, while things like the HIV crisis, those horrific murders of Medgar, Malcolm, Martin, the never-ending wars, Nixon's impeachment, Kennedy's inspiring deeds, Johnson, FDR, Truman, are distant memories.

"Your choice, Adele. Bra or panties. Remove one or the other."

"David, don't be fresh!"

Then there was June Cheever and her penchant for oral sex. And Rhoda Lane. Tit fucking. I graduated NYU, went on for a master's at Columbia and, somehow, at the same time, managed to work in Harlem. And there were more women. "I'm taking my Masters in Anthropology, David. I graduate Brooklyn College at the end of the year. That's when I'm going to turn my attention fulltime on finding a husband. Do you want children, David?"

The first woman with whom I had something super-serious was a luminous African woman born in Ibiza. She had studied drama at the Obafemi Awolowo University and was new to the city. What I remember about Mumbi Emecheta were her parents. Dignified people. Originally from Lagos. Mrs. Emecheta insisted on chaperoning her daughter whenever we went out in the evening. My friendship with Mumbi ended badly.

It was me. It's always been me.

Searching the collages, my eyes fix on Cantor Lazar. My father never forgot to take me to Mr. Pollock's candy store. We would sit at the ice cream counter. He would throw down two shiny pennies for a pretzel, and when he splurged, it would be a nickel for three. He never forgot to make sure that I got what I loved. That was an extra seven cents for a chocolate milkshake.

My mom yakked a great deal on the telephone. What I remember best is that near the end of her life, when she needed a walker, a wheelchair, and often an oxygen tent, Mom never stopped making those fundraising phone calls, soliciting contributions for the many charities she worked with. Haven't thought much about my mother in these years that have passed. Have been dangerously detoured by more pedestrian concerns, but now, as I'm recalling these yesteryear events, I'm remembering things that I've let slip my mind. Perhaps things were disremembered because of my pathology. That's a word I've abused. And still abuse whenever I'm groping for answers to who I am.

Better off sticking to Mom. She was a professor of psychology at Barnard College for years and years. And then, after she was blind-sided by a Buick coming down a one-way street, she became an invalid, was chained to her bed, she started to work with autistic children and other small fry with speech impediments. Mom was great with children. She had been mentored as a Barnard student by Gordon Allport. Allport was more than impressive in his day for his contributions on personality, psychology, and trait theory. So was my mom.

And so, the question remains, "How did I get to be the fuck-up I am?"

Not every bounce is predictable.

My dad had been a child prodigy. As a boy of eight, Dad traveled the country earning a living, giving concerts, living with strangers, sending home dollars, and when he evolved to manhood, he took over a synagogue of historic repute. He chose a wife, had a son, soon began doing radio on the Jewish Hour every Sunday, performing at garish weddings in magnificent catering halls, the Waldorf, the Pierre, the . . . all those other opulent places where people showed off their money. What I remember as not tacky was the salmon and whitefish and pastries that my father brought home after those weddings.

My father did other things, too. How I loved going to Yankee Stadium with him. Sitting in the grandstands for a buck twenty-five. Doing something that to this day brings a smile to my face. My dad and I chased down baseballs during batting practice. We'd position ourselves in right field. Wait for the left-handed Yankee sluggers to take their swings. We'd jump over benches, dive over the hard wood aqua-colored chairs, ignore our bruises, end up chasing down as many baseballs as we could. I always took my baseball glove to those Yankee games. I must have brought home over 100 American League baseballs during my early years. The Yankee Bombers who hit those baseballs into the right field seats most frequently were Dick Kryhoski, George McQuinn, Gene Woodling, Tommy Henrich, Charlie Keller, Joe Collins, Cliff Mapes and, of course, number thirty-six, the lumbering Big Cat, Johnny Mize. The tobacco chewing Mize was near the end of his great career but still a magnificent hitter. My dad and I officially titled him "The MVP of Batting Practice." The Big Cat's blasts traveled as if in slow motion as they drifted over the 344-foot sign, most of the time three to eight rows deep. We'd be positioned there waiting for them, many times into my glove's waiting web. When Mickey Mantle arrived in '51, his thunderous celestial blasts would soar halfway up the bleachers or to the very top of the third deck in right field. Mickey was not one of my favorite batting practice hitters.

It's 4:30 in the morning. I've awakened from a restless sleep. Tossed and turned most of the night. Kept thinking of my son. Liam's everything I am not. He's the good in my life. Elizabeth is aware of that. She realizes that never once until meeting her, did I have the guts to try to have a committed domestic life. Liam and Elizabeth scrambled my center. My raison d'être for a radically different kind of loving, authentic life: Liam's little feet, his perfect hands, the smell of his hair. Even at sixteen he emanates the whiff of the infant he once was.

July 15th, 2015 was the worst day of my life. I have had contracts put out on my life. Two of them with door buttons down, ugly men in black Lincolns, ready to finish their job. I was never terrified, just living my life. I didn't whine or squeal to those two ugly men. I used my wits, called Solomon Lepidus, and I'm still here. But what took place with my son Liam, that scared the life out of me.

Liam was self-conscious. He hated the way he looked because his spine was bent. Elizabeth started researching and learned everything she could about the problem. Elizabeth even learned medical jargon, scientific reasons. She has the kind of mind that can pick up on these things. She did all the homework that was needed. Our son is everything to us. Our life! The main reason—probably the only reason—that Liam and his mother took a trip to Japan three weeks before his surgery was so that he would be distracted from the upcoming operation. I didn't go. I would have only slowed them down. For me, walking is hobbling. My stamina sucks. I would have screwed up their trip. And one thing I do admit, as perfect as my son is, he's terribly impatient. "Ba! You're not keeping up! Can't you walk any faster?" So, I didn't go. Best decision I could've made. Elizabeth and Liam had a great time. And when they returned to New York, it was time for his surgery.

Squirt was fifteen years old. We decided on New York Presbyterian Morgan Stanley Children's Hospital at 165th Street and Broadway. Elizabeth and Squirt selected the surgeon, David P. Roye, a St. Giles Foundation Professor of Pediatric Orthopedic Surgery at CUMC Pediatric Orthopedic, Spine. That's what it says on Dr. Roye's business card. In real time, let's just say that Dr. Roye is a saint. Never met a humbler human being. A more soft-spoken, empathetic, decent fellow. My son immediately had confidence in him, so did Elizabeth. Dr. Roye wore nothing-to-brag-about ties. He certainly did not look like or carry himself like a Wall Street New Yorker or a Greenwich hedge fund greed-monger. He looked like who he was, a man taking responsibility for helping children on a Triple Crown level. Every day leading up to the surgery was impossible. Small talk doesn't help. Intellectualizing just gets on everyone's nerves. Hollow words, large thoughts, babbling goes out the window. Your child's life is hanging by a crippling cord. You worry! You're frightened! You think of all the nightmare scenarios. Spinal fusion means you must cut bone and meat. Open the back to get to the spine. Put in rods to straighten the spine. My son's spine. Anything can go wrong. Everything! Liam was the bravest of the three of us. He was quiet but determined. He wanted the surgery. He didn't look forward to it, but he was resolved. I don't want to think what he looked like. Let's just say he didn't look like your average fun 'n' games teenager.

After talking about it, thinking about it, worrying about it, going out of your mind about it for 310 days, the day finally arrived. We took an Uber to Children's Hospital. Checked in. Went to the room we'd been assigned. The clinic nurses introduced themselves. We'd already completed volumes of paperwork. Signed all the documents. My wife is good at handling stuff like that. My son also waded through it. He grasped it, nodded his head but didn't talk about it. When it comes to the important things in his life, Liam invariably depends on his mom. I would, too. I'm a misfit. Hopeless, helpless, and just about a nothing male to have around under these circumstances. Elizabeth is the bulwark, the competent one. The one upon whom both my son and I count.

Thank God my wife loves me. Her love for Liam is a given. So are Elizabeth's sacrifices. Her competence. Her going a thousand miles forward and backward and whatever else it took to get our boy prepared for this miserable day. Dr. Roye also prepped us.

Now we're in the waiting room. Liam is silent. Elizabeth and I keep looking at him. Peeking is a better word. He looks nervous. He looks as if his upper and lower lip are fighting one another. It's as if his entire face is at war with his mouth. His mouth is where he is living. No words, just a taut holding-it-in look, blue innocent eyes that keep communicating with his mom. I'm there but not really. It was Elizabeth who was there. And then, an aide appears. "It's time." And my boy stands up. Walks through the door. Out of the room. He never looks back. Elizabeth and I stand up and helplessly watch as our son leaves our jurisdiction and passes into the hands of strangers. We don't say a word. I feel as if the curtain is coming down. All that love, all that time spent bringing him up, worrying about him. Protecting him. Giving him everything you have to give. He's gone. It's out of my hands. You're powerless. You're useless. Liam's alone. With strangers. You don't even know their names.

My son was on the operating table for six hours. All that time Elizabeth's two best friends—Jody and Lavina—were with her (and me) in the hospital waiting room. Both kept talking, providing distraction and love. I'm glad they were there. Both women were great. Are great. They gave a whole lot more than what I had to contribute. I stood in the corner, paced the room, went to the bathroom, and was dying all six of those hours. Then it was over. Liam was finished with that part of the ordeal. Dr. Roye—thank God for Dr. Roye. He got Liam through it, and the painful recovery period began. Four days in the Medical Center with his mom sleeping in the hospital room, staying around-the-clock, with nurses in and out, scurrying around at Liam's beck and call. We took our son to our country home in North Salem, and Elizabeth provided 24/7 care for the next ten days. Liam was in terrible pain at first. Even with the painkillers. Elizabeth was there every minute. Me? I was useless. If I entered Liam's room, he gave me a look. He knows whom he can depend on when things get out of sorts, and it's not me.

Through the recovery period, Liam had more courage than I would've ever had. The pain was rough. The medications not much use at night.

"Don't worry, Ba. I'll get through this. It's hard but think how lucky I am. In six weeks, this will all be a blur. I'll be back at Choate. Looking normal."

It's over now, Dr. Roye. Thank you. When Liam was in the hands of Dr. Roye and his team, I held my breath, "Please, God," I whispered under my breath, "just give me back my son. That's all that I want. Take all my dollars. Just give Liam back to me. He's everything to me!"

CHAPTER 18

I'd rather hold hands with my wife than with any woman I've ever known. I love her honesty, her overall goodness. I'm thinking how we hooked up.

Julie Rizzo called. She reminded me of my line comparing my rooftop streak with women to the great DiMaggio's fifty-six game hitting streak.

"That was inane," I said.

"Yes, but it made me chuckle," Julie said. "My boyfriend and I broke up. I'm depressed. I thought of you. All the laughs we had," Then she asked, "How old are you now?"

"SIXTY-TWO."

"Oh, my God!" she uttered.

Our conversation changed direction.

"I have a friend who has had some success with a dating service."

"I could never do that."

"What if we joined together?"

"My name is Elizabeth Dunn," she said, sputtering.

Elizabeth and I spoke on the phone. Within minutes, I knew that we had a special connection. Sometimes you just do. We arranged to meet.

In front of the door, two cartons of cat food. I winced. Rang the buzzer. Once...Twice...Three times. It took several minutes for Elizabeth to unlock the door. Then she darted back to her sofa. She had the look of an abused woman. I had seen that look when I worked for the Welfare Department. You never forget. "This woman needs help," was my first impression. Elizabeth didn't utter a word.

"Do you want me to stay?" I asked.

Not a peep.

"Do you want me to leave? Do you want to go get something to eat?"

Elizabeth finally stood up. We went to dinner at a Thai restaurant in her neighborhood.

That was the beginning of these past nineteen years. When I took Elizabeth Dunn home that night, she told me, "I've never been happy one day in my life."

When I heard that, something unlocked in me. A river of real emotion. I thought it best not to rush things.

I moved toward the door.

"Must you leave?" she said.

I had never met anyone who needed me more.

When I got home that evening, I raced to my Smith Corona and wrote the following:

> *Elizabeth Dunn reeked of torment. Pressure that kept building and building. There were sealed trunks. Piles of clothes in disarray. No open windows; no fresh air. Nothing but dark isolation. It resonated everywhere. Especially within. Not a moment of peace. Not a moment without pain. Not a second of let-up. Elizabeth Dunn functioned in a minimal way. Each social function dreaded. Each victory pyrrhic. Each momentous step forward causing exhaustion. Her body didn't lie. Mutilation everywhere. The inability to do the big things. The little things. Everything for Elizabeth Dunn was overwhelming. There was no place to go. Nowhere to escape to. No door to open. Puritanical shame wherever you looked. Nothing came easy. Everything was hardscrabble. Everything Elizabeth accomplished was courageous. Every defeat crushing. The crucible she carried was from yesterday. And yet, the largest sadness was in the present. It was me. When I walked into Elizabeth's life, I could not adjust to the mutilation. My raised eyebrow, grimace, my value judgment—imagined or real—what was the difference? Elizabeth Dunn felt my reproach in every increment of thunderclap silence. My invisible wincing complaints. I could not sweep away what*

was there any better than I could hide what wasn't. I was not pure of heart, but I was pure in my wanting to help her. I could not help her at first. She could not help herself. She lived with her wounds. The wounds that were still screaming inside of her. She heard my criticisms before they were uttered. And they were never uttered. She could feel disapproval though there was only praise, concern and compassion. Her throbbing pain seemed endless.

That was our first date. Elizabeth was thirty-one; I was sixty-two. In those days, I was still telling everyone that I was ten years younger. I didn't tell Elizabeth the truth for the first three or four weeks. Elizabeth was unwell. I was her first male experience since her breast cancer surgery. She was terrified.

The one thing that I was always able to do was babble.

I'm a babbler. I'm boorish. I'm egocentric. At times, I can be obnoxious. I know my flaws. What did I babble about?

Mostly Jessica, Leslie, Debbie, Amy. How did Elizabeth respond? With nods and shrugs. Sometimes, with an expression of doubt. Sometimes, a word here. A word there. Sometimes she bit her lip or wrung her hands or touched her knee or just sat opposite me on that scratched up blue leather sofa with her three cats on her lap, frozen. That's how it went for the first three or four months. Why did I stay? What made me keep returning? I felt needed. I felt something I hadn't felt in a very long time.

"Elizabeth, maybe you're right. Debbie Turner might have been correct for being disappointed in me. I can see that now. The more money I made the more depersonalized and disconnected I became."

Every once in a while, I'd stop, give Elizabeth a chance to get a few words in. Ask her what she thought. After our first couple of months together, she had a strong opinion on whatever it was we were chattering about.

"David, do you have any idea how much time you spend talking about those women from your past? And you describe each one of them as a ten. It's enough already, understand?"

As Elizabeth began to relax with me, she would say a lot more than, "David, I need to feed the cats."

And then, in our fourth month together, Elizabeth started to almost give me a smile. A quick kiss now and then, sometimes a brief hug or a light touch to my shoulder. We didn't go out much. One of the few times we left Elizabeth's apartment was that first date when we had dinner at the Thai restaurant. After that, we went to maybe four or five movies. For the most part, we would just stay at her place and talk.

Elizabeth is almost six feet tall, a totem pole. Intense wide-set blue-green eyes. Cheekbones like Vanilla Ice. What was she like at the very beginning? A character in a gothic tale. Gaunt and harrowed. What attributes did I perceive in Elizabeth on first look? She had distress on her brow. Pain in her lusterless stringy hair. There were patches of skin visible on her scalp. She would break into tears if I as much as mentioned, "Tell me about your family." She'd start to shake if I inquired on anything close to intimate. She had a mournful countenance 24/7. A voice that seemed to almost be crying. Still does. There was an enormous quantity of self-consciousness. She seemed to have a coiled electric current running through her body. She was always covering up her chest. Clasping her elbows. Her forearms. Rocking. It made me feel as if she were a bleeding, gushing, open wound. And that proved out. We remained strictly platonic. Believe me, Elizabeth Dunn was not an ingénue. No way. Yet, she had sand, earth, and grit in her. Not anything less than a complete wound of a person. She was as authentic as winter can be when it's igloo cold. Our friendship evolved from, "I've never been happy one day in my life" to become so much better than sexual treasures with Leslie, my happiness pill days with D.T., Amy Cho's lyrical yoga chants and sweetest of nothings, or all the money bags I've buried.

It took Elizabeth a long while before she was comfortable with me. She would hold my hand, which for me was wellbeing. When we attended films, I would put my arm around her shoulder. Anything more just didn't take place. And then, one day, somehow, miraculously, I broke through. From then on, the two of us were chatterboxes.

"David. Tell me about your handicapping. Start from the very beginning."

"I started back in 1970 when I was at the Department of Welfare taking home less than $200 a week and had moved back in with my parents. I owed a ton of money. I started to think what it was that I

kosher salt into which I put his store-bought teeth." I paused. "Nathan Rubin always had a crease in his trousers, and that crease could cut you." I stopped again. "I never loved him like I loved Solomon Lepidus, Liz, but I respected him a whole lot more."

I would climb Elizabeth Dunn's flights of stairs just about every other night. She lived on the top floor. Each time after catching my breath, I would tell her about my life.

"Elizabeth, did I mention to you that I visited 52 East 118th Street? I was curious to see if a former client of mine was still living there. Gabriela Blanco. While I was in the neighborhood, I also visited the Meleta Marquez Family Center. I arranged for hot meals to be delivered to East Harlem families from 124th Street all the way down to 97th Street."

"What made you decide on that particular area? And who is Gabriela Blanco?"

"That area was the territory that I covered when I did casework in Harlem. Fifty-two is one building I'll never forget. That holds true for Gabriela Blanco as well."

Fifty-two East 118th Street. Fifty-two! It was the most ravaged building on my route. Probably in all East Harlem. A week doesn't go by that I don't think of Gabriela Blanco. She was thirteen years old, eight months pregnant. She had a sweet face, tulip lips. It was somewhere around Christmas time, circa 1970. I was doing my job. Making field visits. Evaluating client needs. Trying to help. I ended up at 52. I was on the top floor of the walk-up.

In those days, I didn't huff and puff when I climbed stairs. I was standing in the hallway with Gabby Blanco, proud, actually beaming, because she had just finished telling me, "I heard you, Mr. Lazar. I'm going to return to school after I have my baby, Mr. Lazar. I'm determined to change my life." We were standing in the hallway when two addicts came out of nowhere. They began shooting at one another. Gabby and I were in their crossfire. A third male was also there. He was inebriated, started laughing as he watched the commotion. I lifted my field book to my chest. But Gabriela didn't have a book. Bullets sprayed the hallway for what seemed like the time it takes for the Red Sox and the Yankees to complete a game. The gunfire was short-lived. Both men cut out. Ran down the stairs. Disappeared. Gabby wasn't hit . . . or was she? She gave me a look that said, "There ain't no hope." She then entered her grandmother's railroad flat and slammed the door. The inebriated spectator had been struck by a bullet. His chest was gushing blood. I raced to his side. Took out my handkerchief to press against his wound. In seconds, my handkerchief turned completely red. I took off my belt and used it as a tourniquet. "Don' fuck with me, whitey!" he said. "I might be beer drunk but I ain't H high. Besides, my old lady will be here any minute. She's taking me to the Joint Disease Hospital. I have a date with the electrolysis machine over there. Got two bad kidneys."

"The thing is, Liz. I was already a veteran caseworker by then. I took it all in stride. Quickly leapt down the flights of stairs two at a time. Reached the street. Headed for the nearest subway thinking that I must remind Debbie Turner to make sure to always carry her black field book with her when she goes to the field. That thought hit me because I noticed a bullet embedded deep in my thick field book." I peered at Elizabeth.

She had the same gaga look that Debbie Turner had that day at the Welfare Department when I assisted that woman in the intake section.

"Did you find Gabriela Blanco?"

"Yes, I did. Just about nothing left of her. She had five children. Three of them are in prison. The other two are twins. They left New York City when they were in their teens and got involved in the drug business. They're somewhere in Los Angles. Gabriela said that they are doing okay as far as she knows, but she hardly ever hears from them. That's as much as she told me. What's even sadder is that she's still receiving public assistance."

"Elizabeth, Amy Cho was the only woman I had a long-term relationship with who still likes me."

"David, now you're exaggerating."

"Did I tell you that Amy's getting married? After all these years of being alone, she's finally found someone. I'm happy for her."

"So am I, David. I honestly mean that. Amy sounds like the kind of woman who didn't get much out of life. I'm glad for her."

Elizabeth and I started having dinner together every night. As far as I was concerned, Elizabeth needed me. Every now and then, I couldn't help myself from showing off.

"Swan Lake was a big flop in 1877, Elizabeth. It wasn't until Marius Petipa and Lev Ivanov choreographed it anew that Swan Lake became what we know today. For your birthday next week, I'd like to take you to see Swan Lake at the Met."

We became friends, best friends.

"You're my closest friend, David. I must ask you something important. Right now, I'm scared of going further. Does that bother you?"

Whenever Elizabeth asked direct questions like that I froze. I was sixty-two-years old. A four-time loser. Elizabeth was half my age. I felt I had very little to offer. What would I say if she told me she wanted to have children? And I felt that if I came on too strong, Elizabeth would run away. I tried to downplay my feelings. I didn't have the courage to go after her full throttle.

"David, I might be thirty years your junior, but let me tell you this, you're a very complex man. And in some ways, I'm beginning to think you're a coward."

Talking is good. Talking is great. Talking with the right person is just about everything. I'd climb those six flights almost every night. And even though I was in generally excellent health, I had a hard time climbing those stairs. By the time I reached Elizabeth's door, I'd be about ready to collapse. I think that was something Elizabeth liked about me from the get-go: how much of a he-man I wasn't.

Every time I was with Elizabeth, I spilled out more truths. Not that I claim any eloquent insights. Elizabeth had the real acumen. Certainly, more common sense and groundedness than I had ever had.

During her early years, she was home-schooled by her mother. She later went to a middle school that graduated only sixty-two percent of its senior class. Then she went on to the University of Tulsa, but that's not what's important. No more so than Elizabeth being a Presbyterian.

Elizabeth Dunn is a witch. There isn't anything I ever say to her that she doesn't grasp before I am able to finish the sentence. There isn't a novel that I recommend that she doesn't immediately read and immediately comprehend. There is never a conversation that we ever had to which she doesn't add something super-discerning and insightful: from women should have equal pay to civil rights issues to why she believes that Justice Ginsburg is the most liberal judge on the Supreme Court to who's going to win an Oscar to why *Oklahoma* is the greatest American musical of the twentieth century. All these years with Elizabeth and I'm still advising everyone we meet that when my wife expresses an opinion, she'll always back it up with an earful of intelligent reasons. And when she talks about the musical *Oklahoma*, she'll sing the Laurey Williams role as if she were Shirley Jones.

"Tell me more about your mother," she said one night.

I did, and as sometimes happened when I spoke to Elizabeth about my mother, my eyes welled up.

I told Elizabeth that I had done unforgivable things, but the one thing that haunted me most was not being there at the end of my mother's life.

"You must think of me as an a-hole, and perhaps I am. I admit at times that I am unencumbered by values or conscience, but not all the time. I could rationalize by telling you that traffic being what it is in Manhattan, a yellow taxi would've been bumper-to-bumper from Columbus Circle to Madison and 59th Street, then going north for thirty-six blocks, it would have taken a lifetime.

"When my father telephoned me that day, it was 2:45 P.M. I had made the trip to the hospital dozens of times, and it takes a minimum of forty-six minutes to get to Sinai. 'Fatty' died at 3:01 P.M. You figure the percentages. It was NO BET."

Years later I would tell people about my cold heartedness. Nathan Rubin cackled dry and shrill. "I'll tell you Sonny, I was an orphan. I don't know much about that kind of stuff." Solomon Lepidus grunted. "I know it was a case money bet for you, Davy boy, but still, it was your mom." Amy Cho turned white, said nothing. Debbie Turner exclaimed, "I don't understand you—" Leslie said, "If it were my mother, I would have done the same thing."

Elizabeth said, "You were a different man back then."

I wanted to tell Elizabeth my bottom-line truths. Not what friends, family members, and others believed, but what and who I was. I wanted to spell out the vicious things I had done.

Confess.

Every time I climbed those arduous stairs to the top floor, I wanted to.

Every time I reached her door and took a deep breath, I was about to.

Every time I entered Liz's apartment, I knew what I wanted to say.

During our first year together, I didn't speak in much detail about my handicapping exploits. Most of my experiences were too damn toxic.

"Bruno collected, Davey boy…" Solomon Lepidus removed his thick glasses. "What the hell, Davey boy! Stop being a choirboy. Ressler's fortunate that's all he did!"

Solomon Lepidus stopped speaking. It was time for me to stop asking questions.

"I take full responsibility for that part of my life, Elizabeth. The truth is handicapping and making illegal money were never things I was proud of. One good paragraph I write is worth all the dollars I made gambling.".

"David! I'm not upset. I'm trying to think of your handicapping prowess as a special gift. Like a boy being six foot ten at fifteen. That boy has a chance of being a hoop star if he applies himself."

So, I had a small gift. I applied it to handicapping. Made money. Not by today's standards, of course. Today, those one percenters are involved in billion dollar deals.

"What I wanted to tell you, Liz, is that it was rough when I lived with my parents. Even today, I can still see my mom's purple blotches from diabetes."

"David, I'm sorry to interrupt you but would you mind if I made some suggestions about the novel you've been working on? I've read the first hundred pages. I think no one is going to read it unless you give it a more coherent chronology. You must tell your story with a linear construction and connect the dots so it'll make perfect sense to the reader. Otherwise, the reader will get lost."

"Elizabeth," I say, seething as I do, "risky plotting is contemporary."

"If you're not concerned with your novel being successful, do it your way."

And Elizabeth started pounding away at me as if I was on a losing streak.

On each of our dates, I became more and more impressed with Elizabeth. She had common sense. Was obviously a woman who would enhance a lover's growth, progress, and creativity. The point she was making about my Leslie Kore novel, well, it was valid. I began to think about continuous flow, and right in the middle of that, I excused myself, raced home to my Smith Corona and focused on a sliver of text that I was going to insert to make it more to Elizabeth's liking.

Two days later, I climbed those flights of stairs. Liz was waiting for me at the door.

"Tell me why you despised Leslie so much."

"It's not easy for me to talk about this stuff, Elizabeth. I've always blamed Leslie for everything bad that happened in our marriage. It was so much easier then—" I paused. "Elizabeth, I've never spoken to anyone about this before."

"What is it?"

"This is difficult for me to say. Not to you. To me. You know how I always tell you the best thing I've ever done with my life was reinvent myself each time I found it necessary. That's not exactly true. With Leslie, it wasn't that I had a need to leave or to reinvent myself. It was my own paranoia that destroyed us. What I'm trying to tell you is that it wasn't all Leslie's fault. The truth is she was never aware of how I felt. Imagine living with someone you feel murdered your baby. That was me! I didn't think it was crib death that took our daughter. I felt it was Leslie. It's difficult for me to confess this even now, Elizabeth. I could have lived with Leslie's bigotry. Her contempt for my writing. My refusal to make a better living. With everything else that she was freaking out about. What I couldn't live with was my feeling that Leslie murdered our baby. They say one thing leads to another. The money issues. Working in civil service. My guilt over Jessica. My gambling. My writing. The police knocking on our door every other day. One fight after another. Living the way we did. We were never compatible. All we had to give each other was our lust. Leslie had the kind of demonic madness that turned me on. She never stopped competing. That's not even the correct word. What I'm saying is—she was my demonic equivalent."

"You're not making sense. I have no idea what you're trying to say."

"I'm trying to tell you that I'm not like I was with Leslie. After we divorced, Leslie remarried. She went from shrieking 'Gambler!' to being more specific. Once Leslie started to give me rational explanations as to why she was so unhappy with me, I began to see her side of the coin."

"I understand, David."

"No, you don't. That's the story I tell everyone. It wasn't anything like that. Even Leslie thinks it was. It wasn't." I stopped. Took a deep breath. "I never once thought of our infant as an obligation. From the day our daughter, Heather, was born, I loved her. Leslie, on the other hand, had told me a hundred times, 'Having Heather is not something I'm looking forward to. She's going to make my life miserable.' And Leslie never relented about our money issues, my working uptown, my gambling. As I said, one thing leads to another. We were such a disaster, that even Solomon stepped in. He offered me a shot at managing one of his sleazy clubs. 'I'll even throw in twenty percent ownership, Davey boy, if you turn it around and make me a profit.'

"'No, thank you,' I said, 'I'm not going into the pole-dancing business.'

"Then he offered to introduce me to Leon Mancuso, who'd started out as a bookkeeper in 1929 for Clinton Concrete and became chairman and chief executive officer. 'Leon's good people. I'll talk to him, Davey boy. He'll start you off at a really good salary. Within five years—seven at the most—you'll be a multi-millionaire.'

"'Working with concrete isn't my dream job.'

"Solomon tried. He even hooked me up with his sister. She and her husband owned one of those portable toilet companies. They placed toilets on construction sites all through Staten Island.

"'Solomon, I'm not going into the shit business.'

"Whatever Solomon tried to do for me, I turned down, Elizabeth. All legitimate opportunities—hell, great opportunities for anyone—but me. I wanted to be a novelist. Working in Welfare for me was like an actor waiting on tables until he gets a break."

"I still don't get it, David."

"I always had the feeling that Leslie was responsible for our daughter's death. I couldn't shake it. I know now that's not true. But that's how I felt. And because of that, I never gave Leslie a moment's peace. I'm not even talking about love or affection. I'm talking about peace."

"What changed?"

"I came home one night and found Leslie in the bathtub. She had slashed her wrists. Can we drop it now? I still have trouble talking about it."

"David, I have one more question."

"What is it?"

"Are you now who you want to be?"

Elizabeth and I would talk for hours. For me, it was a catharsis of sorts. For her, it was new beginnings. By now, we were going into our second year. I made every effort to make sure that she knew exactly who I was. I knew that I didn't want to fail. I had failed enough.

"David, your generation has a real problem with living life on the ground. Love isn't splendid. It's hard work. It's sacrifice. When two people get together, it's not always a many splendored thing. It's clogged toilets. It's an everyday plumbing chore. My dad worked for the fire department when I was young. He was disabled on the job. The department had to let him go. Being a fireman was all my father had ever wanted to be. After his accident, my mother had to take over. And she did. My father was never the same. He'd stare out the window all day. When I came home, he'd smile at me as if nothing was wrong. Everything was wrong. We lost our house. My big sister got pregnant. Left home. My younger brother took up with some bad dudes. Got into serious trouble. He too disappeared. My father was an invalid. But somehow, my mother managed to keep me in check. I got through high school and, after that, I got my college degree. That was only because I worked two jobs. And one of the deans looked out for me. My mother worked a trillion times harder than me. My dad, well, he smiled and tried to be there for us, and, in some ways, he was. He was a very brave man. Ask any of the men he worked with at his fire station, but, after my brother disappeared, my dad withdrew into himself. Sort of vanished. And then, one morning, his heart stopped. Just like that, he was gone. My mom died, too. Cervical cancer. I've been on my own for a long time, David. Now I've had this setback, but the doctors tell me I'm almost all better. Life's been hard for me."

"Elizabeth, I've been thinking. Maybe you should move in with me. And don't worry about being frightened because of you know what. I'm more scared than you are. It might not occur to you, young lady, but I'm soon going to be sixty-three. Every time I think of going into the bedroom with you, I get frightened. I mean, about the way that I'll perform. Maybe both of us are cowards in similar ways. Maybe both of us must learn to trust each other. Start to laugh more. I think one thing is true for sure: neither of us are anything like Leslie Kore. That's a win-win for starters."

"That's also true with your late friend, Solomon, David. I hate to say this to you, but I think your friend—whom you believe walked on water—was an evil man. If we're going to live together, you must promise me that you'll give up your romantic notions concerning that man. You'll have to start living an authentic life. I'll do my part. You must do yours."

"I'm ready."

I'd been traversing this swirling earth for sixty-two years, definitely in a fog. Then I encountered Elizabeth Dunn. Once her health was restored, what emerged was the strong woman that she is today.

"Elizabeth, I'm not going to lie to you. I'm not saying the money I made means everything to me, but the truth is I never looked at myself the same way once I started living my life as a handicapper."

"I know you like talking about all the money you made, and that's all great. Nothing wrong with being proud of professional accomplishments. But the secret to you continuing a successful life and feeling good about yourself is to do what you're passionate about. That means working on a novel. Writing for you is a whole lot more important than handicapping or sleeping around or buying a Maserati."

I had put on twenty-seven pounds doing absolutely nothing. I was going to the movies, the theater, watching TV, taking long walks, over eating, spending money like water. All of it should have made life damn good. But it wasn't enough. Elizabeth, before she became my wife, took me out of my sloth and prodded me back into a life worth living. The fact that Elizabeth became the centerpiece in my world made it all the better. Maybe that's what I should be telling Squirt, that his mother reinvented my life.

One morning in the middle of breakfast, Elizabeth set her coffee cup down and reached for my hand. She started to ask the kind of questions that in the past I would have answered with boldness, a spontaneous blindness to the other's regard. At this advanced and mellowed age, I was domestically trained to euphemistically answer just about anything.

"Why me?" Elizabeth asked.

"What do you mean?" I said.

"You know what I'm asking. All night you were ranting about that 'happiness pill' of yours, Debbie Turner, from, what is it, forty-five years ago or such? About how much you loved her. How happy the two of you were from the first day you met. How it wasn't Debbie's fault, but yours, that she left you. Well, David, if you felt that why, why is it you let her leave?"

I didn't let Debbie leave. I raced after her. As Solomon Lepidus' wife told me more than once, "David, you've been walking around on tip toes for six months now. It won't happen. You will never get Debbie back. She's gone. If not physically, then on an emotional level, she doesn't feel anything for you"

I desperately tried to get Debbie back. We both tried. You know what she said after six months of trying? "The plug has been pulled. There's nothing inside of me. I have nothing left to give to you." And she went on and on between sobs telling me why there was nothing left to give. I looked at Elizabeth.

"I'm grateful I learned how to love a human," I said. "With you I'm different. Sometimes I don't recognize myself." I paused. "I'm so different than the young man that I was. Cruel, dumb, reckless. I thought I was God's gift . . . You know what I mean. I loved Debbie, and she loved me, but I treated her as if that was enough. It isn't. Every day I tell myself that unconditional love is a figment of the imagination. A relationship needs tenderness, caring, sensitivity, thoughtfulness, awareness of the differences between two people. It doesn't matter if you're an identical twin or conjoined at the hip. People are different. Each one of us an individual. Each one of us needs vigil, awareness, keen ear-and-eye that allows the other to be a person, an individual, and you must be cognizant of that reality. When it came to Debbie Turner, I treated her as if she were my conjoined twin. That was my mistake, Elizabeth. I didn't listen to Debbie." I paused, took a deep breath. Then said "I love you, Elizabeth, but hopefully I never forget that you're your own person, separate from me. An individual that I love completely, but at the same time a person, a strong, independent woman with wings to fly away like Debbie Turner did. Fly away and never return."

And after saying that, I didn't have any other eloquent words to add, no other emotional framework or context for the bombardment to continue that had just rained on Elizabeth. I think my wife got what I was trying to say. I know it sounds like gobbledygook, but, on the other hand, I think it also sounds like what it is: the confession of a dumb man who had lost everything and learned his lesson. I am acutely aware that I got lucky once again and found what I was looking for. Thank whomever, I found Elizabeth. I'm holding on. Not giving her up. And that's what I was trying to convey that morning.

Later in the same day, Elizabeth spoke to me again. "One thing that made me sad was that day we were making love, and you told me the more you went over your life, the more you realized not how much it meant but how little it meant." She squeezed my fingers and raised her cup for another sip of coffee. "The other thing I'll never forget is that when I asked you what the best of times in your life was, you told me working on a book. Starting with a blank page. Being surprised by what you wrote. That was the very best that you had to offer, and that's when I fell in love with you, David. I was sure I knew exactly what you meant. At least I think I did."

Then she held my hand in both of hers.

"I don't have the words to say this right. I don't read like you do. I can't come up with reference points or authors like you do, but I do know that I find flashes of some of the positive things you're saying every time I walk in a children's playground or look into a shimmering lake or up at the blue sky or at city people just scurrying around in Central Park. When you start gabbing about the enormous contributions of eighteenth- and nineteenth-century Russian authors, my mind wanders, yet I realize it's your way of telling me something I think I already knew deep inside. I think that when you say the best about you is a blank page to fill up, what you're truly saying is you're trying to replenish your life with significance through possibility. That without possibility, life is seriously diminished. What you were bereft of wasn't wealth but what all of us so desperately need: a way to feel that we have something pure to strive for. Something that would again give us the feeling that life is worth living. What I love about you, David Lazar, is that I'm sure til your very last breath you'll be trying to fill that blank page. Do you understand what I'm saying?"

"You're telling me two things, Elizabeth. One is that you want me to work on a novel. And that I title it *Possibility*. The other is one day you would like to have a baby. And that we should call it Possibility."

"David Lazar, I love you . . . I love you."

CHAPTER 19

And not long after, Elizabeth said, "What do you think about us having a baby? And, David, honey, before you answer, know this: It's important to me. I really want a baby, your baby. Think about it. Don't answer me now. The only thing I ask is for you to be honest with yourself and with me. If it doesn't make sense to you. If it's too much of a sacrifice. Hell! If you think it's too much for you to handle, we won't do it. Either way, I'm not going anywhere."

Some weeks later, I took the Metro-North train up to Ossining, New York, to visit Sing Sing. My friend, Anthony Marcello, is rooted there with an eighteen-year sentence for manslaughter. Marcello was reputed to have been the biggest bookmaker on the east coast. He was the one bookmaker that I considered a close friend. Of all the men I have known, Anthony Marcello was the guy I would want with me in a foxhole. For years I had been corresponding with him. Long personal and biographical letters. In return, I'd receive brief, up-to-date communications on how bad the food was at Sing Sing. How the only thing he had to look forward to were the "trailer visits" with Gloria, his wife of thirty-two years. She'd come for two days with enough food for six people, and the two of them were allowed some privacy away from the correctional facility's principal grounds. I was in the minority in my belief that Marcello was innocent. Most law enforcement officials believed that Marcello belonged in a cage for life.

"Antony, the one thing I never forget is the first time Elizabeth and I spoke on the phone. 'My name is David.' 'Hi, I'm Elizabeth,' she said. After seven minutes I told her I felt we had a special connection. 'I think so, too' she said. Another thing that still holds true is when I hold Elizabeth's hand. It's everything: You know all that B.S about the sex Leslie and I had. It means nothing next to holding Elizabeth's hand. It's as if our souls are touching. Don't look at me like that. I mean it. It's more than I could have ever asked for." I paused.

"Anthony, I didn't want to tell you this in a letter. I wanted to tell you in person."

"What are you saying? Not the RICO people again?" Marcello stopped. "Who died?"

"No, nothing like that. Elizabeth is going to have a baby."

Marcello's face broke out into a big smile. He jumped to his feet. Kissed me on both cheeks. "That's the best news I've heard since my daughter told me the same news. You'll be a great father, David. I'm gonna pray for you."

Marcello paused. Waved a finger at me.

"It's a smart thing you did, Davey. I mean, walking away from handicapping. You don't need to put that kind of pressure on yourself any more. You'll see. This thing you're doing. Turning domestic. It's a good thing. You're going to love being a dad."

When the eavesdropping guard moved on to another inmate's table, Anthony Marcello's face turned grim. His watery eyes connected with mine.

"Lazar," he whispered, "you made a lot of enemies before you retired. Many of those nasty boys are still mean, and too many of them are still around. I don't want to have to send your wife a bouquet of flowers or a fruit basket. Stay retired. Have a son."

By the time I left Sing Sing's gray and grime, I had the feeling that I could handle being a father.

"Elizabeth, I definitely want this baby. Elizabeth, stop crying. You know I can't take it when you cry."

We brought Liam home in an Afghan blanket when he was two days old. He was tiny, tiny, and he looked up at me and smiled. That first week, every night, I'd extend my thumb. Liam would hold it tightly until dawn. Right away, I knew that Squirt was everything that's good in the world. Squirt has always been that to Elizabeth and me. Liam might have fierce temper tantrums, but he's honest and intelligent and thoughtful and such a good boy that on Parents Day at Choate Rosemary Hall, all his teachers compliment him effusively when we visit. Liam studies without being told. He is an activist for human rights—civil rights, women's rights, transgender rights, and a ton of other rights.

"Ba, I'm aware that civil rights were a giant issue in 1963, but are you aware that economic justice and civil rights go together? White working-class people and civil rights will only become one when we trust our president. What we need is a president who stops talking to his donors and starts talking to the people. Ba, why are you looking at me like that? What's wrong?

"Nothing, Liam, nothing at all."

The only complaint that I have about Liam is generational. He doesn't read enough. As a teen, I read voraciously, but I never did a tenth of the good deeds that Squirt does. I know it's only a father talking, yet, in my opinion, Liam is perfect, both inside and out. He's an all-around decent kid. I repeat this often, but sometimes the best thing in your life needs repeating.

When Liam was five, I'd race him every morning to the 92nd Street Y preschool.

"Don't cheat, Ba. I'd rather lose than have you fake it so that I win."

At fourteen and a half, I had to give Liam up.

Elizabeth said, "Liam has a choice. He got into Dalton, Horace Mann, Collegiate and several of the other Manhattan private schools. But Choate is a great school, and I think it's important that he become more independent."

Liam said, "I don't want to go to school in the city, Ba. I loved Choate when we visited."

It broke my heart.

Liam is the purest love of my life.

It's three in the morning. I have sand in my eyes. My cataract surgery was successful, but both my eyes have been itching since then. There are so many things you just learn to live with when you get older. I got up because I had to pee. I try going back to sleep but all I do is toss and turn. I dwell on an argument I had with Elizabeth earlier this evening.

"I'm guilty, Liz," I tell her. "I am not any different from Solomon Lepidus and all the other guys that I rubbed shoulders with. I fired my own gun when I had to. It was a war. I didn't go to Canada. I wasn't a conscientious objector. I didn't surrender my arms. But Evan Strome got away with his larceny just like I got away with mine. I estimate that he buried at least sixteen extra-large industrial trash bags filled to their bloated brims with $100 Franklins." I stop and stare at Elizabeth.

"Go back to sleep, David. I love you."

"I love you, too," I say and close my eyes.

Early the next morning while my coffee was brewing, I placed a brief epistle under Elizabeth's pillow:

> *Without you, Elizabeth, my days, months, and years would be as unrealized as my life would be without words or ideas or books, it all goes together for me.*

Of course, that won't answer Elizabeth's question about Evan Strome or about the others, but it reminds me of the terrible cost should I decide to be honest with her. And if lying will further corrode my soul, is that a price I must pay for staying together? A price I'm willing to pay?

Liam is home for the weekend. I take advantage of that to tell him some truth.

"Liam, the dollars I made handicapping never came close to the contented and fully alive feeling that working on a novel brings me."

"Ba, you're just saying that because you don't want me to make those kinds of mistakes."

"Liam, you're smart, serious. You care about people. You'll never make those kinds of mistakes. More and more, you're evolving into the man I want you to be." I gaze at my son. He's almost as tall as me now. His face still had acne blemishes, but it doesn't blind me from seeing what a good-looking boy he is. His intelligence, too, is visible. In his eyes. On his brow. Like his mother's.

"Liam, you'll be in college in a few years. Once you step onto your college's campus, I promise that you won't have to listen to any more overbearing rhetoric from me. But for now, trust me when I tell you that you're perfect. I'm not just throwing out kudos. I'm proud of you. Of course, I'm aware that you can make just about every important decision on your own. But let me at least believe a little longer that I still have something to contribute. I still need to feel needed."

I walk over to my desk and take out an old scrapbook in which I had listed special moments in Liam's life. Losing his first tooth. A multitude of teacher comments all the way back to pre-kindergarten. A photograph of him receiving a prestigious Brotherhood Award in the eighth grade at Cathedral. Laudatory comments from current Choate preceptors. Pictures from birth to now. His sonogram. A thousand other memories stuffed into this scrapbook. I slowly look through them. Peel away one page after another. Slowly read my notations.

Liam sits next to me. Places his arm around my shoulder. "I love you, Ba."

How much truth do I dare to tell him?

For of all my carrying on about Liam's many strong points, I still have my fatherly worries and concerns. Liam has never had a sip of beer. His friends have. He's just so damn straight. Forget about taking drugs. That will never happen. He's always the first one back in his room after a dance, and he's never once caused grief to any of the people in charge. In all my son's years, not once has he ever given his mother or me a single thing to worry about.

And that I'm worried about.

Everything goes two ways or three or four. With Liam, junior year has been rough. Liam's perfect because there's nothing he doesn't have. The best thing about Liam is he never stops trying. He's aiming for MIT or Georgia Tech or one of those other engineer universities. I know, they're challenging universities, but Liam has been programmed for that. The thing is I didn't give him street fiber, the ability to kick ass out of defeat. He got a sixty-seven on a math test this week and he's freakin' out. I told him, "Liam, if you tried your hardest and that's the best that you can do, then it's okay. I'm on your side, son, and if you don't get into an engineering school, that's okay, too. There are one or two hundred other schools out there that all have great campuses, top professors, and pretty women."

"You don't understand, Ba!" Liam screamed at me. "I'm Liam Dunn Lazar! I can't get a sixty-seven on a math exam. I can't go to some crappy school! I just can't!"

I don't give a fuck if Liam goes to Harvard or Yale or if he ends up at a community college. What I want is what I told him.

"Liam, lighten up. All I ever wanted for you was to be happy and healthy, to like yourself and to always do the best that you can. The rest of it is B.S. Reach down deep inside yourself. Fight like hell. If you want to join the Sanitation Department, that's okay, too. Whatever your gut and brain tell you to do is good enough for me. I'm on your side. I'm not going anywhere, and neither are you. So, get your ass back to your desk! Talk to your math teacher. Maybe to Dana Brown as well." Dana Brown's the student advisor at Choate. She's the kind of person who sees things for what they are.

Elizabeth is exhausted by all this drama. Me? From now on, I'm going to dig in and listen more carefully to Liam. My take is that not everyone's destined to be an Einstein on every exam. These privileged kids at Choate and all those other one percent of one percenter schools, what do these schools actually do for you? As soon as you have to reach down deep inside, when you hit rock bottom, where are they then?

"It's up to you, son. I'll always be here for you, but it's up to you and what you have inside of you. And that doesn't mean that you have to be number one or number one thousand and one. Just reach down deep inside and figure out what you can and can't do. Start out with a $25 bet and try to build on that."

"Ba, you don't understand!" Liam's exasperation with me resonates in his tone. "Ba, that was your generation—it's different today." He shrugs. "Oh, forget it! That's just not how the world is anymore!"

Elizabeth is still fast asleep. I don't want to disturb her, so I tiptoe into the den. I want to say something profound to Liam. Something all-knowing about life. I can't come up with anything at all. For some reason, I keep turning over in my mind the first day I met Noah Weldon, when we were fourteen and starting out at Commerce High School, and then Leslie Kore flashes in front of me. I can see Leslie at the NYU frat party standing in the middle of the dance floor wearing a powder blue sweater, a navy-blue skirt, a pearl-colored blouse with a heart-shaped pendant around her long neck. Leslie's cheeks were apple red, her hair chestnut, her long legs enticing, and she was flirting with at least a half dozen feverish fraternity boys. I stood in a dark corner ogling her, yet I felt we were destined to meet. Of course, Leslie was incredibly beautiful, but there was much more to her than that. Leslie Kore was everything I had ever dreamed a woman could be.

Enough of this. It's not helping me with, "What can I tell my son?" All I can think of is what every joker always says, "Life goes too fast." With all the things I've done, all the outlaws I've known, all the books I've read, all the illicit adventures I've experienced, none of it seems to mean very much. Who hasn't had a sliver of a proper/improper life? What does it really mean? We all end up gone. I've now crossed out thirty-eight of the forty-one people that have been good-to-great friends of mine. There are only three left. I had to X out Leslie Kore and Amy Cho this month. Leslie's death was expected. She'd been struggling mightily with Parkinson's for the past two years. Amy Cho was going over her wedding plans at her kitchen table when she toppled off the chair. She was dead before she hit the floor.

Amy was only fifty-five.

One month later, still reeling from funerals, I lost another old friend. I received a phone call from Annette Stiloski. "Big John" had passed.

I'm remembering that night when Elizabeth confronted me about "my women." We had grown close, and it was scaring her. I knew by looking at Elizabeth's face that it was coming. She was more conventional than she let on. Her values were not "old school" but they weren't digital either.

"Why have you failed miserably in every relationship you've had?" Liz named the women. "Do you have a clue as to what you did wrong? Have you grown since then?"

"It's easy to say that I've changed. But something always gets in the way."

"I'm not judging you. I'm only asking. It's troubling me. I'm frightened. You've lived a reckless life. A self-indulgent life. I'm half your age. You seem to have little capacity for settling down."

"I can tell you that I've changed, Elizabeth. In some ways, I have matured. I'm more self-contained. My body has slowed down. I want different things today than I did in the past. I want someone to share my life with, not only because I have a yen for her but because I'm more capable of long-term thinking. I don't want adventure. I no longer need to be a workaholic. I don't hunger for More! More! More! I'm not empty inside, I'm full. I want to experience what we have to share. I want to enjoy my life with you as a partner I believe in. Who I know isn't going to leave. Someone who can be with me and independent of me. What I'm trying to tell you is you're the woman I want to share the rest of my life with."

I stood there, my hands hanging at my sides. Elizabeth looked at me. Squinted. Then stood up straight and slowly walked into my arms. And then, I think, we were pretty close to one.

CHAPTER 20

I'm not "the man I use'ta be . . . " No, I'm a whole lot better in most ways. At least I think I am. Being an ex-newspaper guy, I should stick to the facts. Like this one: each day I get more domesticated, weaker, and stronger. Still, I'll never be as good in this role as I was at handicapping college basketball, but I certainly love this job a whole lot more. Just the other day I scooped up two dozen African bracelets made of colorful beads from a Nigerian woman peddling them at Columbus Circle. For the most part, all I did for the past two days was hand them out. Many of them, right now, are at The Smith being worn by Becky and Monica and Kyle and Cameron and Nicky Azzara. I've also given one of these bracelets to Albert Rolon, my building's top-gun handyman, and I've given these colorful bracelets to several of our doormen, and Barry English, our deskman, and Jenny Kelly, one of the building's administrative assistants, and Gerry Welsh, our tenant manager, also to three of our porters. You can see them on Tim Brown's wrist, the grey eagle, at the Porterhouse Steakhouse and Jennifer from Kingston, Jamaica, who works at the Duane Reade and Jose Lopez, the La Mode Cleaners' delivery guy.

The third day I went over my checklist for the people I wanted to give bracelets to. After all, there are thirty-one men that work for my building, of those thirty-one there are at least twenty-four that I'm more than familiar with. They're more like distant relatives or high-school buddies, men from the Dominican Republic, Puerto Rico, the Philippines, China, Cuba, Brazil, Senegal, Poland . . . Let's say these men are a melting pot of people who work terribly hard to earn a small salary and survive from one paycheck to the next. On this checklist is Hector Cabrera, a decent guy, speaks limited English, hard-working, always willing to do special chores for me on my rooftop, from planting trees and bushes to pushing monster planters over the three thousand feet of rooftop space I have. Yes, it's quite a park I have and I couldn't maintain it without men like Hector. Hector's a high-character guy, loyal, more than loyal, the kind of fellow who if you treat right, to use Solomon Lepidus' lingo, will take a bullet for you. One hour later, I discover that the Dominican porter has a problem. In broken English, Hector struggles to tell me: "They've taken blood tests, Mr. Lazar. Doctor tells me I got something called Crohn's disease. I have to receive chemo treatment, I won't be able to work."

"How are you going to pay your rent?" I ask. Cabrera has four young children, supports the woman he resides with. His take-home salary is twenty-seven-hundred-a-month.

"I don't know," he says shakily, almost embarrassed, as he tries to explain his predicament.

"Are you going to be collecting Disability Insurance?"

"I think so. Management helped me fill out some papers. Miss Welsh said she thinks I should be getting $691-a-month."

I thought about it for a second or two. "I'm going to do this Hector. I'll make up the difference between your disability benefit and your lost salary for the time you can't work."

Hector Cabrera remains silent. Then utters a sob: "You're better to me than my father ever was, Mr. Lazar. My father never helped me like you do."

I glance at two medium-sized photographs on my wall. The one I'm looking at right now is of several mature men. These guys are laughing, telling tall-tales, eating like gluttons. For years, Stickers, The Colonel, Rodney Parker, Solomon, Amy Cho (during the time she lived with me) religiously attended my Sunday brunches. We all marched onto my rooftop and shared our fellowship from 11:00 A.M. until approximately three in the afternoon. Then, the women in these men's lives would start pestering them with phone calls or some professional obligation would jump into the mainstream, and we'd lose each other until the following Sunday. Those fun gatherings took place, a rough guess would be from the time I was thirty-seven until I was fifty-two. That's about right because Amy Cho broke my heart when I was fifty-one, and when I was fifty-two, Solomon Lepidus died. Without Solomon Lepidus around, our brunches lost a whole lot of zest. When Solomon would show up, he'd march into the kitchen, unwrap the salmon, whitefish, herring, and whatever else he'd purchased at Barney Greengrass or Murray's or Zabar's, and he'd go straight to work. Nothing made Solomon happier than scrambling eggs and having all of us compliment him on how great they were. We were real bonhomie friends. We liked each other. No mean-spirited Blondies in this gang. No envy or anger or betrayals toward any of the things we did apart from each other nor did we pay much attention to each other's accomplishments or putdowns and, believe me, there were many of each. Our group was made up of self-made, earthy New Yorkers, men who did something with their lives. Most times shady; sometimes sunny. Many times, Solomon would invite an outsider who was just as much a bona fide New Yorker as we all were. There were times Nathan Rubin joined us, rarely his son, who was at the time in charge of Nathan's cable company.

Nathan Rubin, like Solomon Lepidus, had several unlawful businesses, and once I shook hands with those two moguls, I became connected.

Stickers was not one of them in that way. But he was in other ways. Stickers was opinionated, dissimulating, and always promoting. Many times, he brought over one of his new discoveries or veteran artists.

Rodney Parker would also bring over some of his friends, NBA basketball players or scheming coaches looking for high school players and willing to come up with the necessary cash to get them. Some of these guys were household names. Don't let me leave out the original material girl. Madonna came over once when she was a young woman breaking into the business. Surprisingly, when it came to men, Madge, at least to me, seemed clueless.

"I haven't met a man who piqued my interest since I left Michigan, David . . . That's the truth! Not one!"

"I don't want to sound rude or crude, Madge, but did you ever think that if you dressed less flamboyantly it would make a world of difference? Don't take this the wrong way, you're really good-looking, and it's obvious you're extremely intelligent. But as far as presentation goes, well, most men in Manhattan, I mean the kind that you should be dating, are looking for, well, again, I'm not trying to be rude, but they're looking for someone less intimidating. And with the way that you present yourself, like some hippy who doesn't take baths, it would turn most guys off before you had a chance to turn them on."

"Let's just drop it. I'm not interested in your opinion. Furthermore, I like who I am."

Stickers couldn't get Madonna a record contract at the time, but just six months later, Madge broke big because of the musical arranger, Jellybean Benitez.

I sound as if I'm stargazing or bragging, so I'll quit with the Page Six stuff. The mainstays at these brunches were mostly men with whom I'd shared my life. One was Donny Hall, a former high school All American, who disappointed as a player in Division One hoops and yet was still good enough to be the point guard on a Top Ten team. When Donny graduated college, he went into legit theater and became famous as an actor. Donny was a friend of mine for years but then started drinking. I tried to help him with his problem and with his lost career, but I failed. Donny got pissed off at me for failing, and we split because sometimes you just can't put the pieces back together no matter how hard you try. Morty Lefko, The Colonel, was one of our gang. He was a graduate of Morris Evening High School. The Colonel worked his entire life. He started out selling bottles of cheap perfume, and, by the time he was on my rooftop for bagels and lox, he was putting together deals for helicopters and jets. The Colonel took a bath every morning from ten to noon. "Sylvia!" he'd yell out to his wife, "Can I please have a fresh cigar while I'm taking my bath." And later in the day, "Sylvia, these ashtrays need to be cleaned out." Whenever I mentioned Leslie's powers, The Colonel would immediately start chewing his Havana. "I understand what you're tryin' to tell me, David," he'd say, and begin grumbling about his wife of thirty-plus years. The Colonel bellowed a great deal, but we all knew he was good-hearted and harmless. We chuckled at his élan. So did Sylvia.

Early this morning, I woke up with a splitting headache. I knew that if I went to my typewriter and began writing whatever came out would be psychobabble. I wanted to prevent that, so I tried thinking of my twenty years with Elizabeth. I couldn't. I kept leaking and spilling and confusing this present life of mine with the previous one. Sometimes they merge. Sometimes, like when I'm taking a business trip to get some buried dollars, this happens. It also happens when I see women that remind me of other women, women that were in my life, women that are probably now deceased, but still as alive in my mind as the ones I'm seeing right now. I guess this is psychobabble, what I'm doing. It's exactly what I want to avoid.

I begged Solomon's wife to put a phone next to his ear on Thanksgiving, 1989. Solomon was much too weak to talk by then. I told him how much I loved him, despite himself, and how much he had meant to me. I'll always be thankful to Mrs. Lepidus for allowing me that moment.

Everyone's best friend died in his own bed, with only his wife, his children, Stickers, Amy Cho, and me at his side. Amy stifled a sob. "I loved Solomon so much. He was always earthy and friendly, strong and generous. He was simultaneously calculating and unknowable . . . like you are, David!" Amy hesitated. "Solomon would look at me and I knew what he was thinking, and, yet, I knew he would never betray you."

I learned so much from Solomon Lepidus, things hopefully, that my son will never have to learn. As for Solomon's wife, she had to sell off whatever assets she had, relinquish the Fifth Avenue condo in bankruptcy proceedings, move to Florida, survive day-to-day.

Not Solomon. He lives in my mind as large as ever.

They were beaten. They were maimed. Those suckers who took proposition bets from Nathan Rubin. Rubin thought of me as "choir boy." A cantor's son. A "sonny boy" with potential. I went from $25 on a game my first-year handicapping to the fourth year of my roll. That was the year that Nathan Rubin partnered with me. He knew I had something, if not the right formula, at least something the others did not have.

Is that me or is the man I am now me? The answer could be as simple as, "I'm both." Yet, that's too fuckin' simple! Two sides, three sides, maybe even four or five. Not many of us are intact. When Rubin died—he must've been eighty-nine at the time—his last words were, "I'm satisfied . . . " Solomon's last words were, "Don't feel sorry for me, Davey boy. I've lived seven hundred years in my seventy-plus."

What will be mine? I think about that a lot.

What will be mine?

Hi Liam:

When I went to the bathroom this morning to brush my teeth, the first thing that I noticed was a photograph of me with two of my business partners:

Nathan Rubin and Solomon Lepidus. Both men died before you were born, Liam. I think of them every day. And today, I've been regretting that they never had a chance to meet you or Mommy. They would've liked the both of you. On second thought, maybe not you. Like me, they would've wanted to talk baseball, baskets, and boxing. They weren't football or soccer guys and could never have even imagined that soccer would become an American sport as nowadays. But if I told them that you were the kind of boy you are, they would've paid attention. Nathan Rubin would've called you "a sucker." Solomon would've grinned and, Liam, Solomon Lepidus had the widest grin and the broadest face of any man I ever knew. Solomon was the man who tried to buy the Yankees, Liam, for $8 million when $8 million was a lot of money. He lost out to George Steinbrenner and, truthfully, because of his nefarious deeds. He was a man who carried with him a whole lot of baggage and, in this case for sure, his reputation preceded him. With his hunger for power, more power and still more power, he would now be scheming to buy Facebook or Amazon.

Yesterday, Liam, I missed you a great deal. So, at two in the morning, I moved my butt into your empty room and slept in your bed for a couple of hours. It did the job. I felt you were with me, and I felt better. I told that to Mommy, and she's doing the same thing right now. I hope that it works for her as well.

Love you, Squirt.

Elizabeth has been going to war. She's become a Flying Tiger, like that WWII fighter plane. Liz is making a supreme effort to lay down the law. The new edict is no milkshakes! No ice cream! No pasta! No butter! No bread! No pastries! No! No! No! My wife has demanded that I lose twenty-seven pounds. I am following orders. Feel blessed that she cares. My life is a prayer come true. I'm getting up there. When did the bull in the China shop disappear? How is it that I'm ending up exactly as Leslie Kore would have wanted me to start out?

I cleaned out a desk drawer. I found this letter.

> *Dear Ba:*
>
> *I know it seems like I really don't care. Ma probably thinks I'm just writing this because she told me to. I would hope that you of all people can tell the difference.*
>
> *What you have given me is unique. Thank you for showing me that there is more than money and power and grades and exams and school. I am just beginning to realize how fortunate I am. That I am responsible to help those less fortunate. Again, as I get older, I realize how rare this knowledge is. I always thought these truths were just part of me. I was sure you thought so, too. But now I know they were born out of the perspective you gave me. A perspective that is almost always lacking in the money class I was born into. I sincerely hope you never feel you haven't made your mark on me. Father's Day is for appreciation, and I hope this letter at least shows that. However, I wish I could thank you more for all you have done, but I know this pursuit is pointless. So, I'll just close by saying I love you, Ba.*

Liam will be visiting this weekend. When he arrives, I'll insist on hugs, and, when I kiss my son on top of his head, I'll be getting a whiff of his long curly blonde hair. I can't think of anything I'd rather do than hold my wife's hand, get a whiff of my son's beautiful hair.

I'm coming at this from a million angles. I'm trying to throw out as full a picture of my life as I can. Get to the gist of what went on. Focus on the essentials. At my age, it's so much easier to throw out a loaf of bread and try to gobble up the crumbs. Like the way my father fed those Riverside Drive pigeons. He'd tear off a large chunk of bread, break it up into tiny pieces, and toss those pieces all over the place. The pigeons didn't complain. They flew right over, even perched on his shoulders. Started gobbling.

The year I quit handicapping, 2006, I won over seventy-four percent of the games I wagered on, one of my best seasons ever. But I was still ready to walk away. And I did. Today I'm surer than ever that it was the correct decision. I was such a big winner because I took every dollar seriously. Managed them as if I were at war with Adolph. Remembered Nathan Rubin's suggestions.

"Ya see, kid, before making a large wager, I found it helpful to place on my desk the amount I was betting. It sobers you up. Pukes out whatever gambling furies are still inside of you. And always remember, kid, home courts and shorts will keep you in the game."

Sometimes I lose my train of thought. Eighty isn't thirty or forty or even seventy. I jump from both sides of the mountain at the same time. I just don't have the kind of focus I had all those years ago. I've gone to most of the places I've had to go. Looking back rather than ahead is weird, but there is a whole lot more sail in my past than in my future. I'm trying to cut away the lard. Or as Elizabeth says, "My husband doesn't like to talk, but he never stops talking."

How often I feel my life has been a waste of time. Of course, not this last cycle with Elizabeth and Liam. Liam is the best of times. Our communication has evolved.

"Liam, I had my first girlfriend when I was just a bit older than you are now. I think I told you about Sheila Tronn. What I didn't tell you is that there was a rule I had to follow. My hands never went under her shirt or past her waist."

Elizabeth has been a lifesaver. But the rest of it, I would never tell anyone that they should think of me as an example of how to live their life. I'm not despairing. I still have a good time.

I take Metro-North to Croton Falls. From there, I take a taxi to our home in North Salem. When I tell Elizabeth that Champ Holden has died, I spell out the details. "Champ had a stroke. He was improving, following the program set out for him. Gaining strength. Praying daily with his lady friend. Then he steps into the shower. Steps out. Puts on a pair of jockey shorts, wraps a silk bathrobe around his shoulders. Starts jabbering to his lady. Gets up, walks into the study, and collapses. Eighty-seven-year-old Champ Holden is gone. Not a chance to say goodbye to his lady."

"That's too bad, dear," Elizabeth says and then races to change the subject. "David, the deer have been eating the hostas, ruining the hydrangeas, devouring the arborvitae."

And then, soberly, we discuss Liam's boarding school problems. "What do you think, David? Should Liam remain in honors math—he's really struggling—or should he . . . "

There was a time when I would stand on a street corner until two in the morning arguing with friends about issues that matter. But how many of us really care any longer? No one is bringing the sides together. We're being surgically separated like conjoined twins. Further polarized and pushed further apart ("You're wrong, David; Liam must stay in honors math. How else will he get into the right college?") than ever before.

I'm with Elizabeth in North Salem ten minutes from consecrated horse and orchard turf. This evening, we're going to Purdy's, an upscale one percenter eatery, where most of the diners are more concerned with the menu or their next leather saddle purchase than having frank discussions on political atrocities or income disparities or whatever else is the significant obscenity of the day. World suffering . . . gun control . . . healthcare . . . the rising cost of rubbers . . . rape—you name it, these folks, not unlike me ("Elizabeth, remember, tomorrow morning, to remind me to drive over to Harvest Moon. I want to get those rooster sculptures for my rooftop.") are right there with uni-dimensional, axe-to-grind toxic answers.

It's not that different from when my Central Park South neighbor told me, "Did you know that Mrs. Stein has cancer?"

Most of us just go on with our day. I've done that for years. Now, add to this palette the many other issues that I've been ignoring, disremembering, and I've complicated the picture of my life that I'm trying to paint. Now I hear my dead father, "Have compassion for your fellow man, David. Never forget to forgive."

I'm not the right one to preach. I'm not digging up my illegal handicapping lucre that is buried deep in Westchester County earth to distribute among the poor and the starving nor did I ever pay an honest amount in taxes nor did I provide the D.A.'s office with a correct accounting nor do I ever talk to anyone, including my wife, damn hardly even myself, about the elephant in the room: Evan Strome. I'm rambling on about my criminal exploits, trying to get a better idea of the kind of Steppenwolf I am. The Steppenwolf I forget in my life with Elizabeth and Liam. Until she demanded to know about Evan Strome. I recognize my self-deception. I know it can't go on forever. Still, so often it's easier to ignore my past.

Out of nowhere, I say to Elizabeth, "Debbie Turner had brown hair down to her shoulders when we first met. Now she's as bald as a watermelon and still thinks that Tennessee Williams' 'kindness of strangers' line is the greatest ever written."

"What's your favorite line?"

"I'd have to think on that one, Liz. I guess I'm partial to the one in *Cinderella Man*. 'You're the champion of my heart, James J. Braddock.' It's not only the line. It's the way his wife looks at Braddock while she's saying it. I really believed that James J. Braddock was the luckiest man on the planet because of the way his wife loved him."

"I always tell you you're a softie."

Every morning Elizabeth tests my memory. She insists that it's a good way for elderly people to start the day. I welcome the test. I still have a pretty good memory, I think.

"Tell me the starting line-ups for the Philadelphia Athletics and the Boston Red Sox, vintage 1950."

"Connie Mack was the owner and the manager of the Athletics. In those days, Mr. Mack still wore a straw hat. Sat on the bench in a three-piece suit. Looked like Uncle Sam. He must have been eighty-eight years old by then, and I think by the time Mr. Mack left baseball, he had been in the game for sixty-six years. Quite a man, Cornelius McGillicuddy."

"David, stop being a jerk. Name the Philadelphia players."

"I think Joe Astroth was the catcher. At first base, there was Ferris Fain. A really good ball player and just about as skilled as Keith Hernandez when it came to charging bunts. Second base was Pete Suder. Shortstop, Eddie Joost. At third base was Hank Majeski. In left field was one of my all-time favorites, Elmer Valo. Center field was Chapman—don't remember his first name, maybe Sam—and in right field was another tremendous hitter, Barney McCosky. On the mound was a classy left-hander, Alex Kellner. I once saw Mickey Mantle blast a ball over the 457-foot sign in Yankee Stadium off Kellner. In those days, no one did things like that outside of the Mick. The Athletics also had two other left-handed starters. One of them had had a devastating injury during WWII. He pitched with part of his leg blown off for his entire career!"

"What was his name?"

"His name . . . his name . . . Lou . . . Lou Brissie, that's it! The third was a little left-hander, Bobby Shantz. One of the best pitchers in the game for a while."

"You're doing great. Now, see what you can do with the Boston Red Sox team of 1950."

"The Red Sox were a great club in 1949 and again in 1950. I think Birdie Tebbetts hit .303, and he was the weakest hitter on the team. Birdie was the backstop. At first was Walter Dropo. He was the Rookie of the Year in 1950. I don't remember why the Red Sox traded Dropo to Detroit a few years later, but I do remember that Moose once had twelve hits in a row for the Tigers, which I'm almost certain is still a Major League record. Bobby Doerr played second. He's in the Hall of Fame. The shortstop was Vern Stephens. I think he hit forty-four home runs that year and knocked in 149 runs. And, of course, they had Ted Williams. To this day, the greatest hitter I ever saw."

"Okay, Smarty Pants! That's enough for today. You certainly still have your memory!"

I'm remembering the transcendent gift the day I turned eighty.

The three of us—Liam, Elizabeth and I—were returning from Ridgefield, Connecticut where we had had a splendid French dinner at Bernard's. I use the word splendid as Ridgefield is not New York City. The people here seem more polite than everyday New Yorkers. Could just be me getting older. I can appreciate fine demeanors a lot more now than I could in my earlier days. Elizabeth was driving our Mercedes Benz. I was next to her, marveling at the fresh snow flakes on the grounds, in the woods, clinging to the tree bark, the scarce leaves, the drifts of white on both sides of the country road, and then Elizabeth made a sharp right turn onto Barclay Lane, which registers for the three of us. We would reach our security gate in a few minutes. Liam was getting jumpy. An NCAA game, powerful Duke would be playing his favorite lower seed. Elizabeth was also distracted. It had been a very long day. We'd been welcoming me to the Octogenarian Club since well before dawn. And then, out of the snow-covered woods, crossing the road aren't one, two or even three white-tailed deer—there was a whole herd. I'd never seen anything more magnificent in my life. For a moment, all these white-tails froze. I stepped out of the car. Liam followed. We stood in the middle of the North Salem gravel-speckled road, speechless, as these beautiful creatures slowly walked, one following the other, into the deeper cover. Feeling safe, they stopped at a distance. I embraced this as a blessing, and for another four or five minutes, I was able to enjoy their perfection.

"Being eighty has its advantages," I tell Elizabeth. "If I were still thirty-three and broke, no way would I have had this opportunity."

Elizabeth smiled at me. "Happy Birthday, Mister Eighty!" she softly exclaimed and pecked me on the cheek.

As Elizabeth and I have grown closer, we've had many fun conversations, but more and more what entered our talks was the like of "We have to change the doorknobs, Elizabeth. These old-fashioned screw doorknobs don't work for me any longer. I need the lever type now to open the door. It's much safer."

But Elizabeth and I aren't spilt milk. We still make love listening to the moody guitar of Leonard Cohen's "Anthem" where he sings, "There is a crack, a crack in everything. That's how the light gets in." Elizabeth can never get enough of that song or of Cohen's "Hallelujah." Like most of us, though, Elizabeth is a bit of a tennis shoe. She enjoys our paradisiacal country home in North Salem a little too much. The rolling hills, the green lawns, the caretakers that are at her beck and call, the white Benz that she drives, the heated swimming pool and, as much as anything, Elizabeth enjoys getting away from me. My wife loves having the house to herself. One thing I've learned: From time to time, everyone needs their private space.

"David, why don't you go back to the city this morning? Do some writing, and remember, David, watch what you eat, and make sure you schedule a workout with Maggie Giddens."

Maggie makes a supreme effort to help me stay in shape, but the only thing that really works now is my brain. My energy can sustain for maybe two or three hours when I'm at my typewriter. Then, nothing's left. I'll only have bagatelles to sputter. Eighty does not leave much room for purging bursts, insightful gems, even spurious memories. Eighty is not seventy.

CHAPTER 21

I decide not to sleep over in the city. I want to get back to Elizabeth. I miss her. When I return to North Salem, much to my surprise, Liam is there.

"Ba, I'm planning on going to Oxford this summer. Did Mom tell you about the fabulous courses I've signed up for? Did she tell you that my French teacher has us reading Jean-Paul Sartre and Simone de Beauvoir? You know, how I figure it, Ba, that's where it all started for you. Thinking that being an existentialist would set you free. With all the famous people you've known, did you ever get to meet Simone de Beauvoir?"

It's tough not having Liam around. I've loved him since the sonogram. Liam's seventeen. Obviously, he isn't looking back.

I'm back in the city, maundering over what to tell Elizabeth about Evan Strome. Hiring him in the first place was stupid-dumb in two ways. One was I didn't listen to my instincts. Two, I didn't listen to my mentors.

One night at Solomon's restaurant, I told him, "I hired Oscar Strome's son, Evan, as a beard. He's going to school in the Midwest, and I need someone in that area. He's a sharp kid, Solomon."

Later in the week, I received a call from Solomon. "What's doin', Davey boy. You want to know something, Davey boy, just ask Nathan Rubin. That Strome kid is not trustworthy. Rubin has a soft spot for Strome's father. He's been pals with Oscar for a long time. But the kid, he's bad news. 'Do not hire Evan Strome,' Nathan Rubin said. He left it at that. But for Rubin to tell me that much means the kid's more than a winter blizzard. Take it easy, Davey boy. Got to get to a meeting."

I made a visit to Nathen Rubin's Park Avenue home.

"The kid's too ambitious and a steamer, sonny boy. He worked for me when he was a kid. The first quality I can abide. I was the same way at his age. But the second one, being a steamer, that has been the downfall of a lot of guys in this racket. They throw good money after bad. If they lose a bet, they double the next one. Eventually there comes a point when you're desperate, and rather than be a hero and walk away, you become a coward and end up taking a piss on someone else's turf. You know what I mean, sonny boy? If you don't, you'll find out if you stay with Evan Strome."

I was stupid. I kept telling myself that it was my own fault. I kept steaming.

Elizabeth voice on the phone gives me a welcome respite.

"David, Liam texted. He's got a three-day weekend. He's going to bring some of his classmates to North Salem with him. Why don't you take a break and come up here, too? I miss you, David!"

Elizabeth's advice made sense. Going on like this was lame.

The following morning, I call her.

"Elizabeth, you know what I was thinking last night? That we should build a safe room in our basement. I mean what happens if someone breaks into the house? You're up there alone so much of the time."

"David, stop worrying. I'm fine. And we just spent a fortune installing a state-of-the-art security system. Tell you what, I'll drive into the city next week if you promise me that you'll come up here this weekend. Oh, you won't be seeing Liam. He and his friends had to cancel. Something about going to a party he just can't miss, but we can spend some time alone together. And next week, I promise, when I come into the city I'll hold your hand. That always calms you down. I love you, David. Have a great day."

The "have a great day" feels like steel wool in my ear. Yet, I say that I will take Metro-North up to North Salem on Friday afternoon. The truth is I am disappointed about not seeing Liam.

I found an uninhabited bench at Metro-North station. Sat down. Started reading *The New York Times*. I had missed the train for Croton Falls by two minutes, would have to wait for the next one. Fifty-two minutes of catching up with Mr. Trump and other things happening that really aren't happening. Actually, what I'm trying to convey is reading the news of the day is like using toilet paper. Tomorrow the paper will be just as soiled. So I'm sitting at the Metro-North station and this woman slithers up next to me. She sits down. She has sad brown eyes, is wearing a filthy plaid skirt. Her lips are smeared with purple lipstick. Her hair is matted. On her breast is a two-year-old boy, cute as they come. He's sucking on a pacifier as my own Liam did years ago.

The woman is just about touching my shoulder, and as I try to inch away a centimeter or two, she starts speaking, "I want to go to Poughkeepsie, Mister. I have five dollars." She pulls out of a Duane Reade shopping bag a five-dollar bill that she tightly clutches, then waves in front of me. "The homeless shelters in Poughkeepsie are much nicer than the ones here. They're awful in this city. I need twenty-three dollars, Mister. Can you help me?"

Her child doesn't enter the conversation. The little boy seems almost to be a prop. My first thought is, do they let people with babies into homeless shelters? I didn't know. I looked at the woman. Her eyes were bloodshot, as filled with despair as Latoya Earl's were that day when I entered her Wagner Project apartment in 1958. I had known too many women in those days just like that. Too, too many. I can still hear my friend Rodney Parker: "There ain't no hope, Davey. There ain't no hope." Of course, these words by my great friend were uttered to me over forty, perhaps fifty years ago, but I can still hear them, believe them, see them on every NY street. I hear Rodney Parker's voice echoing them right now.

The woman said, "I can make it if I get to Poughkeepsie, Mister. Besides the shelter, the baby's daddy is there." I didn't question the woman. I felt her plight, her pain, her powerlessness. Her obliterated invisibility. Instinctively, I reached for my wallet. Took out two twenty-dollar bills. Handed them to the lady. As I looked into her bloodshot, sorrowful eyes, I asked the woman her name. "Miriam," she said. I reached inside my jacket pocket, that's where I keep my real money. I peeled off ten Franklins and handed the cash to the woman.

"Here's something to start a new life in Poughkeepsie, Miriam," I said. The woman stared at the money before taking it. For a moment, it didn't register. Then it did. She grabbed the wad and within seconds was racing for one of the exits that would take her to 126th Street and Park Avenue. I watched as she and her two-year-old raced down the street. Within seconds, she and her child had disappeared into the Harlem throng.

I'm reading a note Elizabeth placed under my pillow yesterday.

> *Dear David. There may be a younger man. There may be a richer man. There may be a less obnoxious, ego-centric man. But they would not be the most incredible, brilliant, clear-headed, wise, multi-faceted, creative genius you are.*
>
> *P.S. I do know the difference.*

It was written right after one of our very best days.

This isn't one of my best days, far from it, but there has never been a day that I hold my wife's incredibly soft, seemingly weightless hands in mine that the feeling isn't special. It's as if I'm having a sensual experience, a feeling that reaches deep inside of me, that, yes, is sexual, but so much more, more in the realm of true intimacy, that is what I feel whenever I hold Elizabeth's weightless hand.

My eyes are wet. I can't bear to lose this woman.

This evening I wrote to Elizabeth. Didn't talk. Just wrote. You can read what I penned now, but the truth is I ripped it up before she had a chance to read it. Why did I do that? Don't ask. I'm not equipped with a rational answer other than to say I'm a coward.

> *Dear Elizabeth. You are so vulnerable and so strong at the same time. It's difficult to believe all that you are handling and that I, of all people, can cause such distress.*
>
> *I've always been your biggest fan and think the world of you: your totally alive soul, your intelligence, bottom-line values, visceral connection to pain and beauty, your personal admiration of integrity.*
>
> *That said, you are now in distress and have placed much too much importance on my words, opinions, attitudes and spontaneous ignorance. You are your own person. There is nothing to hold onto outside that. Things disappear as quickly as people. In this*

octogenarian's universe people do not disappear—
THEY DIE. What's left are ashes. Twenty-four seven
home care reprieves. Breathing corpses. If you can call
us that. Don't take me that seriously. I stopped believ-
ing in anything other than the moment, Liam and you
years ago. Liz, of course you are important to me, but
you have your own young life, don't screw it up, put
it together as best you can, without my two cents of
interference or ten cents of help. That's how I see it.
If you want to believe that I am all-knowing and can
offer more than that, feel more than that, control more
than that, then you're being romantic, blind, obtuse.
Please, let's stop fighting. As I have written in several
of my books, people are strange, violating animals.
I, too. What is important is what I always tell Liam:
Place one foot in front of the other. Take responsibility
for your own actions. Think for yourself. Don't rely on
anyone more than your own right arm. Make sure you
can summon from deep within the virgin clarity that
you were born with, and remain who you are. That's
great. I'm not.

Today I'm struck by how I see both sides at the same time and how it's paralyzing me. It is the way I've been thinking for some time, as if everything were gray, principles mute, virtues on both sides, not incomprehensible. My comprehension has never been more acute. I'm finding justifiable reasons for each of my thoughts. Everything is fusing. I can defend either choice. I'm going crazy with neutrality. The very opposite is equally dangerous. Somewhere in my brain I keep asking, "What is it all about?" I've never had less certitude. But this new way of seeing with both blindness and clarity makes me feel better than I have in a long time.

Now I feel like facing my decision. One thing's certain, I'm still alive. I had a life. I have a life. I'm still going strong.

For years silence has been my middle name. I told Elizabeth and Liam as little as possible. I buried the truth inside my deepest reservoir of blood and howling. When my every motive and intent was to make their lives better, why tell them things to make them worse, things they didn't want to hear, things they wouldn't, couldn't fathom? It was easier to manage the truth than to tell the truth. I made handicapping sound romantic, made my worldly success sound like achieving the American Dream. I was so much less than the man I presented.

Most people would rather have two cars, a country home, shining-faced children, and a wife whom they love and who knows next to nothing about where the money comes from than to live with debts and a week-to-week paycheck that can run out at any time. Isn't it worth keeping secrets from those you love, who wouldn't be there if they knew the immoralist you are?

So, I told Elizabeth that Evan Strome was a good deal like me. Hungry, good at what he did, and ready to stand up and live a lonely life of secrets so that he could reap money. Greed, maybe, but it was more than money Evan Strome was after. Like me, he lived with a belly rumbling for more. His identity, like mine, needed to prove its worth. If not in a traditional way, then in a way that most citizens disapproved of. For me to judge him as an enemy seemed ludicrous. He did things I did. I'm sure of that. The problem was he started doing them to me.

I had large trash drawstring bags, thirty-gallon capacity, two feet six by two feet nine by 1.05 mil, fits up to a thirty-gallon can. That was not what I wanted. I had Denny Vargas, a porter in my building, find industrial bags that were giant size. Evan Strome did the same. He copied my every move. It was as if I were Lebron and he a rookie learning the game. Strome picked up on everything I did. From numbers to information. From contacts to codes. I didn't mind. He was making me money. He was the most talented and effective beard that I had. If I reached out and needed Evan Strome, he was always there.

"Evan, I need you to get me down eight dimes on Miami of Ohio at four and one half. Don't take less. Can you do it?"

"'I don't know, Mr. Lazar. I'll try.'"

Invariably, Evan Strome came through. I made tons of money because of him.

"Mr. Lazar, I know for a fact that Zack White isn't playing in tonight's Toledo–Akron game. And Toledo's sixth man is out as well."

Information like that, Strome provided. Information even more valuable. Things like finding me half-points in your favor. The difference between winning a wager and losing a bet. Evan Strome was my number one beard.

Then Solomon heard from his friend, the bookmaker Willie Alter, that Evan Strome was screwing me. "Willie Alter opened a Colorado–Iowa State game at six and a half. Strome jumped all over it. But Strome reported to you that he got down at five. What are you going to do about it, Davey Boy?"

I told Liz it took me a week of sleepless nights to decide. I demanded that Strome return the money he had made all the time he worked for me.

"Get out of the country," I said. "Disappear. Your father can't help you. I won't. Solomon Lepidus went crazy when Willie Alter told him how you screwed us. I strongly suggest you disappear!"

I liked Evan Strome. He had been great for me. Made me a whole lot more than a dozen giant-sized industrial bags filled with hundreds. He was opportunistic, motivated to make it, ballsy, sharper than any other beard I had. Maybe as sharp as me.

I told Solomon I got every dollar back. I told him that Strome was no longer living in the States and wasn't coming back. "The truth is, Solomon, I still think of Evan Strome as a reckless kid brother. What was I to do?"

"Davey boy, he's a twenty-three-year old man. But if you can live with it, so can I. Take it easy."

I grabbed Solomon's thick wrists as he was walking out of his restaurant. "Listen to me, I'm serious. Leave Strome alone. He did nothing that I wouldn't have done. He was hungry to make it. You remember those days." That was the end of the conversation.

Elizabeth shook her head and smiled. Once again, I had told her a fabrication. The story was accepted. Our life together was okay.

CHAPTER 22

This is how Evan Strome met his maker. A week later I received another phone call from Solomon Lepidus. He advised me that Strome had fled to Morocco.

"Besides screwing you on numbers, Davey boy, he gave out at least ten of your code names: George Koch. John Brody. Mark Korman. Allie-for-One." I had dozens of code names so that each of my beards could call in multiple bets without the bookmakers changing the lines on me. One beard didn't know the other. I had over 100 beards in my operation, and I kept them disconnected from each other. It was going to cost a lot of money to settle the problem once the bookies found out what I was doing. Money I had made, my partners had made. Evan Strome had betrayed me, often. I did go to Morocco. I did look up Evan Strome. I did . . .

I have this weird feeling. A part of me wishes my son had some street smarts, some street attitude, some of that which I needed to make it. It only comes from having your back against the wall, having nothing, beginning from scratch and a $250 bankroll. That is not part of Liam's experience. Liam has privilege and decency. Evan Strome reminded me of me.

CHAPTER 23

I was in the city when I received a text from Elizabeth thanking me for loving her. I texted back, *The easy part is loving you. The more difficult part is staying relevant in your life. We have a good-to-great marriage. I couldn't have asked for more.* I don't think Elizabeth feels that way, but she does love me.

Liam now has a girlfriend. She goes to a privileged school not far from Choate. How they hooked up, I'm not sure, but both Elizabeth and I think it's great that they did. His girlfriend is more than we asked for. She is competent, intelligent, musical, attentive, healthy, and real. And the most important part of the partnership between her and Liam is that she genuinely likes my son. They have something that I think has a chance of lasting.

I came up to our Westchester estate last night. Now I awake to a glorious day. I get out of bed. Use the toilet. Brush my teeth. Gargle with hydrogen peroxide. Head for the breakfast nook I am most fond of. Scoop the *New York Times* up off the kitchen table. Also, Murdoch's *New York Post*. I feel like puking each time I see the front page of the *Post*. Yet, I enjoy scanning Page Six and reading the sports section, especially Joel Sherman.

Elizabeth enters the kitchen. She's holding her jade-colored porcelain cup of steaming black coffee. Her hands are shaking. The cup is rattling. Liz is wearing my Ralph Lauren navy-blue, cashmere bathrobe.

"I just Googled Evan Strome," she says. "He's dead. He's been dead for years. He died in Morocco, an unsolved murder."

I force myself to remain silent. Not to twitch or flinch. What good would it do to confess? I know what I did. I've known for a lifetime what I did. Who I was. Who I am. I'm the same guy at the Welfare Department who saved that elderly woman's life when she was having a fit. The same guy who rescued Amy Cho. Am I not? Didn't I . . . Am I not . . . I help people. I'm the guy who reaches into his pocket all the time. Didn't I always open my wallet—Damn! I'm sounding as if I'm everybody's best friend. Is that what I've become?

Elizabeth sputters. "Are all these possessions of yours truly worth what they cost you?" She takes a deep breath. "Are these possessions and all your bags of filthy money what you want to bequeath to Liam? Is that going to be your legacy?"

Elizabeth throws up to me things that I've tossed and turned over for just about as long as I've been me. How many nights have I asked myself why it wasn't enough for me to be a caseworker in Harlem? Why it wasn't enough for me to try and write a halfway decent novel? Why it wasn't enough for me to love Leslie?

Debbie?

Amy?

Jessica?

Why was none of it ever enough?

In a scalding and accusatory tone of voice, Elizabeth says, "How many more like Evan Strome were there, David?"

I soon began to throw out some hollow justifications for my actions. "You know how I am, Elizabeth, when I think I'm right, I just don't change my mind. With Evan Strome, I simply didn't want to help him. He . . . "

A large part of me is thinking, "What the hell does Elizabeth know?" Yes, I had reinvented the wheel. Have been playing the family guy. Have kept the proverbial collar around my neck for these past twenty plus years: Domesticated! Loving husband! Good guy! Impressive provider! Exceptional father! I'm certainly a lot more than a gambler! I felt something liberating inside myself that I hadn't felt well, since—I'LL SHOW HER!

What comes alive in me is as filled with the kind of demonic energy that I had in me when I was getting my life together all those desperate back-to-the-wall years ago. The surge of energy that was triggered inside of me back then by . . . Powerlessness! Futility! Paralysis! That's what gave me my rebel's cause, or as I had originally said, the motivation to "make it." To get out of the post office, in a manner of speaking. To rebel! I would've been stuck in civil service my entire life if I hadn't gone to war. I would've been living paycheck-to-paycheck.

I enjoyed being the best at something. For thirty-plus years, I made important money. Squirreled enough away for ten lifetimes. No, make that twenty! FUCK YOU WORLD, I'M FREE!

Fuck it that my life was illegal. Fuck it that I had to do dehumanizing things. Fuck it that I didn't pay taxes. Fuck it that I tried to gain an edge, stay one step in front of the game. Fuck it that I looked the other way! Fuck it that I know of men buried in ditches by men who live in Palm Beach mansions. Fuck it that I can give you a road map to back-alley burial grounds. Fuck all of it! I did it. I lived it. I am it. And this is my ace in the hole. It's the American dream. The proof is that all these years later, I can still count the Franklins that I've concealed from New York to Malibu to the Caymans to Costa Rica to Curacao to Switzerland. I never wanted any part of a normal life. A nine-to-five existence. Saying "Yes, sir," and "No, sir," or paying a fair amount in income taxes. Fuck it that I would never refer to another man as boss, supervisor, employer, captain or Mr. President. Yes, Elizabeth, when you scratch my surface, you're correct, I am pathological and sociopathic, and you can slander me with whatever else you want if that's your inclination. So, love me or leave me, as the song goes. And I rant on and on like that.

"Elizabeth," I say. "I've loved our twenty-plus years. Especially all the years we've shared with Liam. They've been the best years of my life."

Then the game changes. What floors me is not Elizabeth's moral superiority. What obliterates all my rationales, has caused me to bleed, is Liam. My son quietly walks into the kitchen. He heard at least a portion of my self-serving sophistries. I was going to say "justifications." I'm not sure how much Liam had heard, but I know that if my intention had been to justify my actions and not to condemn myself, it flew out the kitchen window. One look from my son. Just one little "Ba . . . !" and I know I'm guilty. Not to the world. Not even to Elizabeth, but to myself. Liam looks me in the eye. I'm guilty as charged. I will never again receive his hugs or kisses. Be able to snuggle up to Elizabeth. Hold her hand. I will never again be embraced by my family. Their moral disaffection will supersede the warmth that we had once shared. I'm not sure if I even fully understand what I'm conveying. What I'm trying to say is that everything inside of me is purged. I'm not even making myself clear to myself. I know that. What I'm trying to tell you is that I felt that my son and my wife not knowing the truth about my life is one thing and not knowing who I really am is another. I'm still not sure which part of me is center stage. I'm as messed up as that. I couldn't say one more word. I was silenced by my own cowardly shadows. What was I other than a poor excuse for a life poorly lived?

"Ba," Liam says.

I look into my son's agonized eyes. He didn't need to say anything else. What is there to say to Liam? To Elizabeth? I never told either of them who I was. My son! My wife! They never knew me.

Elizabeth looks at me. I at her. We do not speak. We do not need words, have words, that could convey her disappointment in me, my evaporation. That's what it seemed like to me. As if I had disappeared, had become invisible, a light turned off, a person no longer breathing. Elizabeth wrung her hands. Those weightless hands that I always needed to hold. She just moved her head slightly, like people do when they want to say "No" but hold the words back. She looked at me with the "How could you?" silence that was so much more penetrating than if she had screamed, screeched, lunged at me with nails and venom. I had held inside of me so much for so many years, so many truths, not only Evan Strome, so many other violations, so much of what I couldn't get out. It's not as if I do not realize my lack of faith in the other, my own insecurities, my rationalized, instrumentalized way of living, an inch at a time, a silent second, a romantic feeling that lasts long as a match might flicker, but what about loving with a whole heart, without secrets, without holding back . . . That's what Elizabeth and Liam were telling me with their silence, with their abstinence. I took it all in, tried to recover. And how does a man like me recover: You already have the answer. He doesn't. He just goes on, waiting for the precise moment to change the moment or the experience or he goes on to the next game. Wasn't it Nathan Rubin who advised me when I was still almost a boy: "When you lose you call your bookmaker up on a Monday and you arrange to pay him. And then you do just that, sonny boy. You pay your bookmaker what you owe him, and then you move on to a fresh start."

Is there a fresh start for Elizabeth and me, crossed my mind. What crossed Elizabeth's mind was . . .

Elizabeth and Liam say nothing.

I find talking about it unreal. I look at my son, my wife, and I know I've said enough.

EPILOGUE
12 MONTHS LATER

One night I reached out and touched my wife's shoulder. Then our hands interlocked. A perfect fit. What we shared was not winning the war in space. Changing the climate. Cooling the earth. But it was something. I smiled to myself.

"Elizabeth," I said, "I love now. Thank you for staying. I love us." My wife slowly removed her hand from mine.

"You're guilty!" she said.

ABOUT THE AUTHOR

PHOTO BY K&R PHOTOS

Robert Kalich is a born-and-bred New Yorker, the city he still calls home. He is the author of several non-fiction books and two previous novels: The *Investigation of Ariel Warning*, and *The Handicapper*, which was a national best-seller published by Crown. Kalich has worked as a social worker, a journalist, and as a professional basketball consultant. He co-founded a film and theatrical production company, The Kalich Organization, with his twin brother Richard, who is an internationally acclaimed author. Robert Kalich is an avid reader and maintains a home library of 10,000 books. He lives with his wife and son in New York City and North Salem, NY.